The Hero Next Door

THE HERO NEXT DOOR

EDITED BY

Olugbemisola Rhuday-Perkovich

  Crown Books for Young Readers

New York

Visit us on the Web! rhcbooks.com

Educators and librarians, for a variety of teaching tools, visit us at RHTeachersLibrarians.com

Library of Congress Cataloging-in-Publication Data
Names: Rhuday-Perkovich, Olugbemisola, editor.
Title: The hero next door / edited by Olugbemisola Rhuday-Perkovich.
Description: First edition. | New York: Crown Books for Young Readers, [2019] |
Summary: A collection of short stories by diverse authors that explores acts of bravery by heroes trying to make the world a better place.
Identifiers: LCCN 2019004431 | ISBN 978-0-525-64630-3 (hardback) |
ISBN 978-0-525-64631-0 (glb) | ISBN 978-0-525-64632-7 (ebook)
Subjects: LCSH: Children's stories, American. | Heroes—Juvenile fiction. | Courage—Juvenile fiction. | CYAC: Short stories. | Heroes—Fiction. | Courage—Fiction. | BISAC: JUVENILE FICTION / Short Stories. | JUVENILE FICTION / Social Issues / Adolescence.
Classification: LCC PZ5 .H37 2019 | DDC [Fic]—dc23

Printed in the United States of America
10 9 8 7 6 5 4 3 2 1
First Edition

Random House Children's Books
supports the First Amendment and celebrates the right to read.

Contents

FOREWORD
by Olugbemisola Rhuday-Perkovich
1

MINNOWS AND ZOMBIES
by Rita Williams-Garcia
7

ONE WISH
by Ronald L. Smith
17

THE ASSIST
by Linda Sue Park and Anna Dobbin
35

HOME
by Hena Khan
59

ELLISON'S CORNUCOPIA: A LOGAN COUNTY STORY
by Lamar Giles
77

RESCUE
by Suma Subramaniam
101

THE SAVE
by Joseph Bruchac
121

LOS ABUELOS, TWO BRIGHT MINDS
by Juana Medina
133

THROWN
by Mike Jung
145

A GIRL'S BEST FRIEND
by Cynthia Leitich Smith
169

EVERLY'S OTHERWORLDLY DILEMMA
by Ellen Oh
183

REINA MADRID
by R. J. Palacio
209

GO FISH
by William Alexander
233

ACKNOWLEDGMENTS
253

ABOUT THE AUTHORS
255

ABOUT WE NEED DIVERSE BOOKS
263

Foreword

"The New Kid" could have been my superhero name. I had a lot of experience with that title. School after school, classroom after classroom, playground after playground . . . I'd swoop in, hoping to dazzle and impress, save the day somehow. Each time I hoped to get it exactly right; each time I got it so, so wrong.

Maybe that's why, right before my first day in a new sixth-grade class, my mom went to the school and basically asked the principal to "put my daughter in classes and groups with the other Black nerds." When I found out, it was a total "MOMMMMMMM!" moment, and I almost cringed myself out of existence. The "other Black nerds" were no less unhappy with the forced friendship. But the parents banded together, as parents often do, and I found myself in study groups and at skating parties with kids who I had much in common with, including a shared determination to have nothing in common with each other. But eventually we got over it. We didn't have a choice. (You know how parents are.) And then we kind of . . . loved it.

We became real friends . . . me, David, Melanie, Shonda, Rob. We laughed and cried and cared about our report cards together. We held each other up; we knew that it was a very bad idea to tell one of us to "calm down." We weathered the storms of middle school because we had each other. Because our parents gave us each other. We were each other's heroes. We still are.

Maybe my mom made that mortifying move because she knew the things I hadn't told her. The secrets that I should have known she'd figure out. Heroes often have special powers—moms especially. Maybe my mom's were knowing the secret pain that I'd held inside my heart, and working to make sure that I had the community to give me the strength she'd known I'd continue to need. Because a few years earlier, for a part of second and all of third grade, I was in a school where there were no other little Black girls like me. Or Black boys. Or Black anyone, for what felt like an eternity. There were white children who chased me out of school, and some who called me the *N* word, their faces red and angry as though my very existence meant the end of the world. I would hold my breath and try very hard to hide how much each day shattered a little piece of my heart.

But in my class, there was also Wendy, who looked at me, and saw me, and became my friend. She was not my benefactor, or my champion—she was very quietly, authentically, simply my friend. I had my parents and grandparents and infinite aunties, who made sure through the books they bought, the toys they made, and the stories they told that I knew that I was beautifully Black and precious in a way that could never be taken from me. Each day, just by their love, they knit me back together again. Heroes.

Sure, I saw heroes in books and movies and on TV, wearing capes, saving the world without their families finding out, stamping out evil with style (and tights that never ripped). Sometimes I played out the fantasy at home, safety-pinning a towel to my shirt and running around the backyard with my arms aloft, and bossing around my (clearly evil) little sister in the name of Good. I had a vivid imagination. (Don't get me started on the time I pretended to be a rhinoceros by sticking two pebbles up my nose.) I thought about heroes a lot—I still do. I mean, we can't really avoid them. Some have physical powers beyond what seems humanly possible; others can think their way into and out of any situation. They're in movies with spectacular battle scenes and jaw-dropping special effects. We use the word to describe everyone from firefighters to mysterious masked figures of legend, from warriors to wizards. From fierce and feisty princesses to the "hidden figures" who change the world without anyone even knowing. We tend to celebrate the larger-than-life icons, the ones who attract the headlines and win the awards, from the activists to the artists, the athletes, and the educators.

Those of us on the margins wonder if our stories matter. I know I did.

And there are the celebrities hailed as heroes whose spectacular, glittery rise is often followed by an equally spectacular fall.

They can be very human, our heroes, not perfect. What does that mean?

Hero.

What do you think of when you hear that word?

Impressive physical strength?

An abundance of bravery?

Supreme selflessness?

We have a million ideas of what makes a hero. We cheer them on; sometimes, soon after, we wish them gone. We wonder about them, ask *why* and *how*. We're inspired and motivated by their magical stories and dream of being like them one day.

Maybe we already are.

In this collection, you'll find tales of ordinary people who do extraordinary things, and the individuals who just might be magic. These are the stories of the risk-takers, the friend-makers, the dreamers and doers. You'll meet a lacrosse player whose mistake might save more than a score, a camp counselor who honors the life in a "zombie's" eyes, two people whose legacy of ingenuity inspired future generations, a girl who sees behind her neighbor's grumpiness the loneliness within, a couple of robot-building twin detectives, a trio of neighbors who tackle a ghostly history that threatens to forever haunt the present. You'll see the power of teamwork with a twist, having a furry friend, knowing oneself, having a special sibling bond; the power of stepping out on faith to offer a second chance, finding joy in a challenge, and the courage to put others first, even when it's scary and you have no idea what will happen next.

These are the stories of everyday heroes in our midst, the ones in plain sight and those yet to be discovered. In ways big and small, these stories motivate, inspire, make us laugh, and, yes, cry. Do you know all the heroes in your life? How are you a hero to someone else? To your community? To the world? It's my hope that these stories remind you of the power you have to speak up, sit down, and stand with, to do and be a hero in your own unique way. You don't need a cape. Or special powers. (Though that would be pretty amazing, right?) Empathy and compassion sound good. A sense of humor can't hurt. A desire to listen will definitely come in handy.

Most of all, though?

You just need . . . you.

Minnows and Zombies

Rita Williams-Garcia

We are the Minnows. Walk-a-Man is a Whale. Daisy is a Whale. All the camp counselors are either Dolphins or Whales, and the campers swim in different schools of fish. When you're seven or eight and need arm floats, you're a Minnow. Next year, when the arm floats come off, you become a Go Fish camper with new counselors. (It's supposed to be *Goldfish* but everyone kept shouting, "Go, Fish, go!" so that school became the Go Fishes.) After Go Fish are the Rainbow Trout campers. Then Salmons. And then the Sharks. The Salmons and Sharks swim in the deep end of the pool. Minnows don't swim past Walk-a-Man, who stands in the middle of the pool.

Today it's a good day to be a Minnow because we beat our relay time. We swam a whole three seconds faster than we swam yesterday. I swam the last leg and kicked as fast and as hard as I could. Usually, Sumaya swims the last leg because she swims fast, but Walk-a-Man told me, "You can do it," so I tried my best. As soon as my hand hit the finish rail, Walk-a-Man and Daisy blew their whistles in a lot of toots. That's how we knew we beat our record and that we earned a treat. All the Minnows went crazy! Not just because we did spectacular, but because we could choose almost whatever we wanted for our victory treats. It's ninety-six degrees outside. We all shouted out the same thing. "Ice pops at Seven-Eleven!"

The best thing about breaking our record is marching to the 7-Eleven on Hillside Avenue for our victory ice pops. The worst thing about breaking our record is marching to the 7-Eleven on Hillside Avenue for our victory ice pops.

Hardly anyone believes me when I say there are zombies in our neighborhood. There are. At first there was just this one zombie and we knew how to dodge him. He was slow. He used to lean against the corner mailbox and reach out his hands as we passed by. He used to have white skin, but you couldn't tell what color his long, stringy hair was before he became a zombie. But you sure could smell him and his stinky pee-pee clothes that were probably never new when he first put them on. It's a good thing we're Minnows and can hold our breath for a long, long time underwater. Although the mailbox zombie is gone and you don't have to be afraid to mail a letter, you can still smell the stinky pee-pee smell near the mailbox. And there are more zombies on Hillside Avenue. An army of used-to-be-men and used-to-be-women block store entrances and sleep on bus stop benches because they are homeless. Then the store owners or the police chase them away.

People feel sorry for zombies and try to buy them food because they look like they haven't eaten. But the zombies say, "No food. Gimme money. Gimme money. Spare a dollar?" That's mostly what they say.

"If you don't want a sandwich," a lady told a zombie yesterday, "then you aren't hungry." The lady did what everyone else did who tried to buy a zombie a sandwich. She walked away.

That doesn't stop them from asking for money. It doesn't matter if you're a grown-up, a camp counselor, a Shark, or a Minnow. Zombies come up to you with eyes that don't shine and they speak slow, slurry zombie talk: "Hey, hey, hey. Gimme, gimme. Dollar, dollar." They don't say *please*. They just zombie blink, zombie scratch, and zombie wait, rocking from one foot to the other. As soon as you shake your head no, the zombie moves to the next person to ask.

You want to be nice to zombies because they used to be real people. Sumaya knows. Her oldest brother, Imiri, got turned into one. He tried to steal her dad's laptop and sell it. Now Imiri can't come inside their house anymore. He had to go away to be turned back into his real self. Sumaya told me she's afraid of him. Afraid of him coming back home. I saw him before he went full zombie, and that was scary. But I don't tell her that he scared me, too. I don't want her to feel bad.

Sumaya isn't my girlfriend. I don't have a girlfriend. She's my swim buddy and my walk buddy. We're the same height, so the counselors pair us together, and I'm almost as fast as Sumaya in the pool. But it's true that she's my friend. She blows bubbles underwater and will probably make a good Go Fish next summer. Out of everyone at camp, I like her the most. But that doesn't mean she's my girlfriend.

We're all dry and have changed into our shorts and tees. And it's nice outside, even if it's nearly one hundred degrees. At least the air isn't so thick and heavy like on most summer days.

Walk-a-Man gives the signal, and Daisy blows the whistle in one loud, short toot.

We walk like a school of fish in our aqua-blue T-shirts. The Minnows walk two-by-two, Daisy behind us, Walk-a-Man in the front. Walk-a-Man taught us to share the sidewalk with moms with strollers and with dogs getting a walk. And with the mail lady collecting the mail from the mailbox. And with the deliverymen wheeling crates of potato chips, snack cakes, and sodas for the 7-Eleven. And with the police officers who get their heroes and coffee from the 7-Eleven. We share the sidewalk with everyone.

Walk-a-Man doesn't have to blow his whistle to get our attention. He gives us the hand signal to share the sidewalk so there's a smooth flow of traffic. He raises his hand up, and then waves it to the left or to the right and then waves it like a moving eel. We step to the left or right, and become one big moray eel! It's so cool! We're like a marching band and we make our two-by-twos into one line to make room for walkers coming toward us. Then, when the sidewalk is clearer, we go back into two-by-twos. It's called courtesy. Walk-A-Man taught us that.

"The important thing," Walk-a-Man always says, "is to walk together, pay attention, be courteous." Then Walk-a-Man does a step and we do it, too. People stop to watch us parade by. Sometimes we high-step. Or we walk, walk, stop. Walk, walk, stop. And when we do our parade and practice courtesy, we don't think about the zombies.

Here's what I figured out: zombies can't high-step. To high-step you have to stand tall. Walk tall. No one stands taller or walks taller than Walk-a-Man.

I don't care what the Sharks say. The Minnows have the best counselors in the day camp. Walk-a-Man is our leader, like "follow the leader," and Daisy is our protector. Daisy cheers the loudest for the slowest Minnow. And Walk-a-Man, whose real name is Walter, says, "Good job," and gets low to give a high five even when you come in last. Walter is Jamaican. Not Jamaica, Queens, New York,

Jamaican, where we live, but from Jamaica, the country. You can tell. He talks Jamaican even when he's speaking English. But he is easy to understand. He always finds time for you. And he's a good explainer. I asked Walk-a-Man, "Why don't the zombies want to eat something?" He said, "They stop wanting food. They are sick. They want other things. Bad things. We can't help them buy bad things."

Sumaya said, "Once they were big and laughed and walked you to school. Now they steal and are skinny, like Halloween bones."

She meant skeletons, but I said, "Yeah." I know she was thinking about her brother, Imiri.

"This is how you know a zombie from a hungry person. One only wants your money."

When we walk down the part of Hillside Avenue where the zombies are, Sumaya squeezes my hand. Like she's afraid. I could go, *Quit it, Sumaya,* but I don't. I feel like squeezing her hand sometimes, too. There are more zombies than there used to be.

Daisy always walks close behind us. She must know we are scared. "Don't worry," she says. "I have your back." Daisy is big, and even though we know she's really, really nice, she doesn't smile at everyone. She keeps her face stiff and serious, especially when we're out walking. The other thing about Daisy is she has sharp eyes. She sees everything, like if you're horsing around in the pool and she blows the whistle loud. And if you don't stop horsing around right away, she jumps in and makes a big splash and comes and gets you, and you lose pool time the next day and have to stay dry and watch while all the Minnows are learning to dog-paddle in the water, and Sumaya gets another partner for the day. Daisy keeps her whistle around her neck, and when she blows it, man, she blows it loud! The zombies are afraid of Daisy, but she isn't afraid of them. She steps up to them if they get too close, and says, "Hey! Get back!" And they zombie mumble and almost fade away.

We arrive at the 7-Eleven. We're all excited and start jumping around. But we calm down because we're about to go inside. Walk-a-Man says we can't go inside until we remember the rules for going inside a store or public place:

> *Walk regular.*
> *Hands to self.*
> *Don't touch anything.*
> *One line, one love.*

Those are Walk-a-Man's rules. Daisy's is simple:

> *Stay with your buddy.*

Walk-a-Man pushes open the door to the 7-Eleven and we follow him. One line, one love. It's nice and cool when we step inside. Sumaya rattles her teeth on purpose to show how chilly it is. We both rattle our teeth and rub our arms. But it's still nice to be inside.

The man behind the counter smiles at us. He sees us every other day. From his smile, I can tell he likes the Minnows. I don't think he likes the Sharks very much. The Sharks aren't allowed inside because of what happened with the Sharks and the candy display. No more Sharks allowed in the 7-Eleven. But we are the Minnows and we're allowed inside.

"Lime!" I shout when Daisy asks which flavor I want. Sumaya says she wants blueberry, then I change my mind. "Blueberry!" Lime tastes good, but it doesn't turn your tongue blue.

Walk-a-Man raises his hands up and then presses them down against the air. "No shouting," he says.

I feel a little small when Walk-a-Man scolds us, but Sumaya giggles.

Daisy and Walk-a-Man always wait until we're standing outside in our two-by-twos before giving us our ice pops. It's taking too long. I want my ice pop now! But we're still inside the 7-Eleven and I know the rules for being inside a store or public place.

I can almost feel the freezing tube of crushed ice in my hands. Even better, I can taste the blue ice on my tongue and feel how it will make my teeth rattle for real and turn my teeth, gums, and tongue blue. Sumaya's, too.

Daisy counts each ice pop as she hands them over to

the clerk. Walk-a-Man takes money out of his pockets to pay.

I can't wait. I can't wait. I can't wait!

But then Sumaya pushes into my side and I am about to say, *Quit it!* but I don't.

I look where Sumaya is looking.

A zombie! Coming down the aisle toward us! He doesn't smell bad but he looks like he is ready to zombie fall on us, so I grab Sumaya's hand and pull her away.

Then Daisy blows her whistle but not so loud, and Walk-a-Man pulls the door open and Sumaya and I start marching, almost running ahead, and mess up our one line, one love, but we have to get away. Daisy tells Sumaya and me to slow down. She stands at the counter with her whistle in her hand to keep the zombie from snatching us. If she wanted to, Daisy could tackle him like a linebacker.

Sumaya and I are glad to get out the door, even though it's hot. Maybe hotter than it was before we went inside the 7-Eleven. Walk-a-Man must feel the heat. When we look up at him, it seems like he's close to the sun. He's so tall. He smiles and calls out the ice pop flavors. "Lime! Cherry! Orange! Blueberry! Grape!" We jump up and down and shout out the flavors of our ice pops. Some of us rub the cold tubes on our faces and arms before biting open the tubes. Sumaya just holds hers. She doesn't even bite hers open right away. She just looks inside at the counter where Daisy is standing.

I look over, too. Daisy and the zombie are at the counter. He looks like he is falling over in slow motion. Just as he dips low, he rises up at the last second, but starts to fall all over again.

Sumaya shouts, "Run, Daisy! Run! Run, Daisy, run!" All the Minnows laugh at Sumaya. But I don't. They didn't see the falling zombie coming toward them in the store. Not like Sumaya and me.

Walk-a-Man doesn't laugh at Daisy. He looks worried, like he wants to go inside to help Daisy, but he won't leave us standing outside alone.

I look at Daisy. She isn't afraid at all. She is talking to the zombie. Then she puts a bottle of water on the counter and gives the clerk a dollar.

Finally, Daisy is safe! She comes outside and Walk-a-Man gives us the signal to march.

When we are far enough from the 7-Eleven, I say to Sumaya, "They must get thirsty, too." I don't say *zombie,* because she knows who I mean. For the rest of the day at camp it's really quiet, even though there's a lot of games and singing and we have our tangerine snack. I think it's because I play with all the other Minnows. But I only really talk to Sumaya.

When it is time for our parents and sisters or brothers to pick us up from day camp, Sumaya says to me, she says, "I miss Imiri. I hope he comes home."

One Wish

Ronald L. Smith

"Got a piece of corn bread, cuz?"

The man's voice was as deep as rolling thunder. Wiry black and gray hair stuck out from under his chin. He smelled like a wet dog.

Sacky looked through the crack in the door. "Not today, Cuz. Maybe when my auntie comes home."

The man tipped his wide-brimmed hat and backed away from the door. Sacky watched him slowly walk down the steps and into the street, then closed the door and made his way back inside.

Everyone knew who the man was. They called him Cuz, which was short for *cousin*. No one knew what his real name was. Some folks said he was a millionaire, and that he had a pot of gold stuffed away in an old broke-down mansion in Selma. Other people said he was so poor he couldn't rub two coins together. Sacky didn't know what to think. All he knew was that the man gave him the creeps, with his lanky, long-legged walk and his odd way of talking. Something about him just didn't seem right.

Sunshine shot down in long rays and bathed the backyard in lemon-yellow patches of light. Sacky sat with his back propped up against the pecan tree. He called it his Thinking Place, but never said that out loud. His auntie Florence said the tree was there when she was born and would still be standing when she was dead and gone. Sacky didn't like to think about that, though. He just liked to eat the nuts that rained down when the crows jumped around in the high branches up above his head.

He reached for a pecan and tapped it against a thick brown root. The secret to cracking pecans was to get a nice hairline crack so you could pry out the nut inside. Smash it too hard and the whole dang shell would break apart and you wouldn't be able to pull out a nice chunk. Sacky considered himself an expert.

His friend Auguster was supposed to come by so they could go fishing. He said he knew a spot in the Alabama River where there were so many blue catfish they'd pretty much just jump right into your boat. But Auguster never came when he said he would, so Sacky just waited and ate pecans and watched the white puffy clouds scoot across the sky.

Sacky woke to the sound of a blue jay making a racket. "Dang birds," he muttered, shaking himself awake. It was just getting to be dark. He must've fallen asleep without realizing it. His leg felt like it was stuck with one of his auntie's knitting needles. *She must be home by now,* he thought. He got up and brushed pecan dust from his overalls, then went in through the back door, which led to the little kitchen. "Auntie?" he called.

No answer.

The house smelled like coal, bacon grease, and yellow cake. Sacky's auntie had made the cake last night, and she'd said not to touch it or she'd whoop his behind. She'd said it was for a church meeting or funeral or some such thing. The cake sat on a platter on the table, tempting him. The smell rose in his nostrils and made his mouth water.

Sacky walked over on his tiptoes, like someone was watching. *God's always watching.* He heard his auntie's voice in his head. *I can just smell it,* he reasoned. *Ain't no harm in that.* He reached out with greedy fingers. . . .

Knock. Knock. Knock.

He froze in his steps.

Who could that be, knocking on the door?

Sacky walked through the place where a door once stood and into the tiny sitting room. He opened the front door a crack.

"Got a piece of corn bread, cuz?"

Sacky sighed. "What do you want?"

"Your auntie home yet?"

"No, she's probably at church."

The man called Cuz rubbed his whiskers and moved his lips around in a slack-jawed face. "Cuz is hungry," he muttered. "You got anything to eat?"

Sacky wasn't sure what he should do. His auntie always said that he shouldn't let people inside the house who they didn't know. But everybody knew Cuz. He was harmless. Or so people said. But still, Auntie Florence never let him in, which didn't really make a lot of sense, according to the Bible.

"You can come in," he finally said, "but just for a while. Okay?"

A gleam flared in Cuz's eye. "Thank you, little sir. Just need a place to sit for a minute."

Sacky opened the door wide and Cuz came through.

Cuz looked around the small room, as if sizing up its worth—the silver candleholders, the good china kept in the cabinet with the glass windows, the silverware from Auntie Florence's grandmother, and for a moment, Sacky thought he'd made a big mistake.

Cuz's eyes finally settled on Sacky. "Let's make a deal," he said.

Sacky screwed up his face. "What kind of deal?"

"I'll give you a wish, if you give me something to eat."

Sacky shook his head. The man was fool crazy. "A wish? What do you mean? What kind of wish? Like magic or something?"

"Some call it that," Cuz said. "Now, let me sit down. My old bones are hurting. Been walking all day."

Before Sacky could say no, Cuz flopped down on the couch. Sacky didn't know how his auntie would feel about that. She didn't let anybody sit on that couch. She called it a *chaise,* whatever that was. Cuz took off his hat and set it on his knee. His shoes were dirty and full of holes. "Something to drink?" he said.

Sacky sighed and went into the kitchen. He opened the little icebox and stuck his head inside. The cold air came out in a mist of white fog. There was a bottle of Coca-Cola, a jar full of corn liquor, some of Auntie's cough potion, and a big block of ice. Sacky took a knife from the drawer and chipped off a chunk and put it in a glass, then filled it with water. He brought it out to the sitting room and handed the glass to Cuz, who took it with long, sharp fingers. Cuz tilted his head back and swallowed it all in one gulp, and then crunched the ice.

"Ah!" he said, setting the glass down on the end table.

"You gotta use the coaster!" Sacky half shouted.

"Coaster?"

"That little round thing." Sacky pointed. "Right there on the table!"

Cuz picked up his glass and set it back down on the coaster.

For a moment, no one spoke. Cuz just stared around the room, like he had every right to be there. "About that food," he finally said. "What you got to eat? I know your auntie's got some catfish and hoecakes back there. I can smell it."

Sacky's eyebrows rose in surprise. His auntie had made catfish and hoecakes the night before. How did Cuz know that?

Sacky had to think. He had two choices. He could give Cuz some food or tell him he really needed to go.

"Old belly's rumbling," Cuz complained, laying a skinny hand on his stomach.

Sacky sighed. "So if I give you something to eat, you said I can make a wish?"

Cuz nodded. "One wish. That's all you get."

"How do you know how to make a wish come true?" Sacky asked. "You know magic?"

"Old Cuz knows all kinds of stuff. People just never ask."

Sacky paused, thinking. "Okay," he said. "Wait here, and don't go stealing nothing."

"Cuz don't steal. Cuz knows right and wrong."

Sacky got up and went into the kitchen again. He took

the hoecakes from a plate on top of the stove and set them on a little saucer with flowers on it. Cuz wasn't getting any catfish. They'd eaten it all the night before. You couldn't just let catfish sit around. You had to eat it when it was hot. Nobody wants cold fish.

Cuz sniffed like an old dog when he saw Sacky come in. "Here you go," Sacky said, handing him the saucer.

Cuz leaned his head over the hoecakes and his nostrils opened wide, like he could inhale the food just by breathing in. "Smells good," he said.

"My auntie knows how to do some cooking," Sacky said. "She's got the best yellow cake in the county."

But Cuz didn't hear Sacky. He was busy shoveling the hoecakes into his mouth. Crumbs and grease filled his beard. He wiped his mouth with the back of his hand.

Sacky sat and watched the man eat. The house was quiet but for the sound of crickets and night birds outside, whistling their little songs. When Sacky's momma and daddy first moved out here, Sacky was only three years old. The earth was dry and flat, laid out like a withered corpse, but they worked a little patch of land and called it home. Sacky was twelve now, almost a man grown. His parents had gone east to look for work and left him in the care of Auntie Florence, who was probably raising her voice in the church choir right this minute. Sacky liked her singing but not all the churchgoing. Folks around here went to church every day and twice on Sunday.

"*Burrrp.*"

Cuz leaned back and put his hand over his stomach. Sacky shook his head. Auntie Florence would throw him out on his behind if he made a burp like that. Cuz reached inside the folds of his coat and withdrew a little silver case. He clicked it open and took out a sliver of wood and began to pick his teeth. He stretched out his legs in front of him. "How about some of that corn liquor your auntie keeps back there?"

Sacky squinted. This was getting to be too much. "How'd you know my auntie has that?"

"Old Cuz knows a lot of things."

Sacky was getting tired of Cuz's demands, but he was curious about the wish. Could he really make a wish come true? There was only one way to find out.

A minute later, Sacky was pouring a small glass of corn liquor into the same glass he had used to give Cuz water. Sacky wrinkled his nose. It smelled awful, like it could burn a hole right through you. Auntie Florence didn't drink it, but offered it to some folks who came by now and then. Cuz drank it down without stopping. Sacky was sure he'd cough and sputter, like Auguster did one time on a dare, but Cuz did no such thing.

"Now," Sacky said, "tell me about this wish."

Cuz breathed in real deep, and then let it out slow. "Need to go outside for that," he said, and stood up.

Sacky had never realized how tall Cuz was, but seeing him rise up the way he did made Sacky think of a giant in a storybook. When Cuz asked for food on people's front steps, he was kind of worn-down and bent, like he carried all the troubles of the world on his bony shoulders. But now he seemed to take up all the air in the room and then some.

Cuz followed Sacky out back. Lantern lights flickered in distant houses beyond the field. The moon cast light down through the weeping willow trees and made the stringy moss shine like silver. Cuz started humming then, a little song that sounded pleasant in Sacky's ears. "What's that song?" he asked.

Cuz stopped his humming. "That's an old song, before the mountains rose up and the rivers got filled with water from God's tears."

Sacky didn't know what that meant. It sounded like some kind of church talk. He sighed and stood in front of Cuz. "C'mon, then," he said. "My auntie's gonna be back soon. If she finds out I let you in the house, she's gonna beat both our behinds!"

Old Cuz must've thought that was right funny, because he threw his head back and howled. "Okay, boy," he said. "I'm gonna give you your wish, but I gotta tell you a story first."

Sacky groaned. "Okay."

"Sit down right there," Cuz ordered, pointing to the gnarled base of the pecan tree. Sacky wondered what old Cuz was up to, but he sat down and rested his back against the tree anyway.

Cuz raised his arms in the air, and Sacky thought they stretched out as long as the tree limbs, but it must've been a trick of the moonlight. "Listen," Cuz started, "for I shall tell you a tale of a dark night, and what happened in the deepest paths of the forest."

Sacky looked up at Cuz. The stars twinkled behind him, and the wind rustled the leaves in the trees. Night creatures stirred in unseen places, hidden.

"Long time ago, when the earth was still young, the wild things were the kings and queens of the forest. There was the mighty lion, with his bloodstained claws, the sleek gazelle, who could run faster than a swift river, and the elephants, whose footsteps sounded like thunder."

Cuz stopped and licked his lips. "And then there was the wolf."

Sacky shivered a little. Something about the way Cuz said that made him uneasy.

"Now, the wolf was sly and quick, and could always find food where other animals couldn't. He found it in the rock caves and in the wide fields, in the mountains and the desert, and one time he found it in a farmer's field."

"What did he find?" Sacky asked.

Cuz grinned. "He found some young chickens. And you know what he did?"

Cuz's eyes seemed to glow in the dark. Sacky shifted his back against the tree. Maybe he shouldn't be out here in the dark with Cuz. "What did he do?" he asked.

Cuz looked left, then right, then straight at Sacky. "He ate 'em."

Sacky swallowed hard. "Ate them?"

"Sure did," Cuz said. "He had a feast!" He shook his head a little, like he himself remembered the occasion. "But the noise of the chickens squawking and clucking sent the farmer out to the coop, and he found the wolf right in the middle of his meal."

Cuz stopped and looked up to the night sky. He let out a big breath. "But this farmer was no ordinary farmer. He was different from the other men, and knew a little something about magic and curses." He paused for a long moment. "Let me tell you something, boy, the wolf picked the wrong henhouse that night."

"Who was he?" asked Sacky. "The farmer."

"His name was Scratch, and he didn't like the wolf eating his chickens. He cornered the wolf with a hot iron poker, and the wolf was so scared he couldn't move. And that's when it happened."

Sacky leaned forward, eyes wide, all caught up in the story. "What happened?"

"Old Scratch put a curse on that wolf. A curse that would last until the end of time."

Sacky wasn't sure if he believed in curses. That kind of stuff wasn't in the Bible, but some people out here swore by it—that somebody could put a curse on you just by saying your name or throwing some dirt over their shoulder.

"What kind of curse?" Sacky asked.

"Old Scratch wanted to make sure that wolf would never have the chance to do something like that again. He wanted to take his life, but he didn't. He took something worse."

A night bug tickled the back of Sacky's neck and he swatted it away. "What could be worse than taking somebody's life?"

Cuz snorted and rubbed his whiskers. "His *soul*. He took that wolf and *changed* him. Changed him into a two-legged creature, never to feel the wet leaves under his feet, to smell the hot blood of the kill, or to sleep beneath the moon at night with his pack. He made him a human man, cursed to walk the earth begging for scraps."

Sacky wasn't sure what was happening. What did this have to do with his wish? He didn't believe this old fool. He was just telling a lie. Nobody can turn a wolf into a man. That was just plain foolishness, his auntie Florence would've said. He was growing tired of Cuz and his lies. "What about my wish?" he asked.

"I'm getting to that, boy," Cuz shot back. "That's the best part."

Sacky leaned back against the tree again.

"Now, this here curse—the only way it could be broken was if a kind soul opened his door to let the wolf in, to feed and comfort him. To trust him. If he could find somebody to do that, the curse would be lifted."

"Okay," Sacky said. "That don't sound too hard."

Cuz narrowed his eyes. "But this curse's got a bit of a snag to it," he said. "Old Scratch made it awfully hard to break. Because the person who let the man in would be blessed with one wish. He'd be able to choose a wish of his own—money or riches or fancy clothes—anything his heart desired." He paused. "Or he could do something else."

Silence.

"What?" Sacky ventured.

Cuz's eyes gleamed again. "He could use his one wish to let the man find his true self. To let him be a wolf again."

The wind sighed through the trees and some clouds passed over the moon. Sacky had a feeling he had just stepped into something he didn't understand.

"Man is selfish," Cuz said, looking up to the sky. "Scratch knew it wouldn't be easy. Everybody wants a wish. But who's gonna give up their wish to free another?"

Sacky drew his knees up to his chest.

"That's why the wolf keeps traveling," Cuz said, "hoping to find an unselfish man or woman who'll give up a wish to help an old, cursed fool."

Sacky didn't know what to say. He opened his mouth, but Cuz cut him short.

"So what's it gonna be, boy?"

"What do you mean?"

Cuz sighed. "Ain't you been listening? I'm the wolf, son, turned into a human man. And I hereby bless you with a wish. Make it one of your own, or let me go back into the wild and feel my four legs under me."

Sacky rubbed his head. *This can't be true,* he thought. *Old Cuz is a wolf?* Then again, his teeth did look rather sharp, and his long legs and nose were quite wolfish.

What if it was true?

He could have all the money in the world. He and Auntie Florence could move into a mansion, and have people cook and clean for them. He could have his own room and toys, get a rifle for hunting—heck, maybe he could even buy one of those fancy motorcars. People said there was one called a Ford Model T and could travel forty-five miles an hour. That'd be a lot faster than a mule and a wagon.

Cuz stood real still, looking up at the moon, and every now and then peering into the woods that bordered Sacky's house. Was that longing Sacky saw in Cuz's eyes? If he was really a wolf, it'd be right cruel to take that away. Sacky thought for a moment. He was in his Thinking Place. Auntie Florence told him being Christian was doing the right thing when nobody was looking.

Then again, what if this was all some kind of trick? *Deception,* Auntie Florence called it. She said that if you kept knocking on the devil's door, sooner or later he'd let you in. Maybe that's what Cuz was doing. He could be working for the Deceiver right this minute.

Sacky bit his lip, thinking. Cuz was still standing, looking up at the stars every few seconds. He'd said that farmer's name was Scratch, Sacky remembered. That was another word for devil.

Sacky closed his eyes. Jesus, he said in a low voice. I'm trying to do the right thing. I know I am your servant, and we all fall short of the grace of God. If I do this thing, please know that I'm trying to be a good Christian. Please don't strike me down with a bolt of lightning.

Sacky blew out a long breath and stood up. "Okay," he said. "I wish . . . I wish that you could be a wolf again."

Cuz's green eyes sparked and seemed to light the dark around them. He ran the few short steps and put his hands on Sacky's shoulders. "Are you messing with me, boy? Are you serious?"

"Sure," Sacky said. "But you gotta promise not to steal any more chickens."

"I do!" Cuz said, and Sacky was sure the man was a wolf now, because he felt his sharp fingernails digging into his skinny shoulders.

"What now?" Sacky asked, a little afraid but curious at the same time.

Cuz didn't answer, only fished around in his jacket and came out with a mason jar, all lit up with light.

"What's that?"

"Fireflies, boy."

Sacky knew all about fireflies. He and Auguster used to catch them and put them in a jar, just like the one clutched in Cuz's hand.

"My night eyes are gonna be old and poor," Cuz explained. "These here glowflies are gonna show me the way to my pack—Fenris and Lobo and Freki and old Yellow-Tail. They've been waiting, all these years."

Cuz slowly began to unscrew the lid. His eyes were wide, and his breathing was growing louder. "Now, boy, I want to thank you for this here deed you done for me. It's mighty righteous, and I'm sure you and your auntie will be rewarded in heaven. But when I say 'Run,' well, you best get to stepping."

"Why?" Sacky asked.

"Because I'm a wolf," Cuz said, and opened the jar. "And I'm gonna be hungry."

Sacky gulped.

Fireflies flew up out of the jar like a yellow twister, lighting up the whole yard and all the dark spaces in between. Then Sacky saw something he'd never forget. Old

Cuz dropped to his knees. His clothes ripped and flew off him as if thrown by invisible hands. And then he raised his head to the night sky and howled. Whiskers sprouted from his cheeks. Fur bloomed along his legs. His back got all hunched, and then Sacky saw the hair spreading over his whole body, but his face still looked like the man he knew. "Run!" the man who was Cuz shouted. "Run, boy!"

Sacky sprinted away, back toward the house. Shadows moved across the moon as quick as running water. The wolf who was Cuz let out one more howl and then darted into the woods, the glow of fireflies fading into the dark.

Sacky stood there a moment, sweating and breathing hard. He'd seen it. It happened. Nobody would ever believe him, not even Auguster.

He didn't want to admit it, but he'd done the right thing. He could've had mountains of dollar bills, candy canes for Christmas, and some nice church clothes for Auntie Florence. They could have eaten fresh venison and ripe fruit till the end of their days. But he gave it all up to give a man another chance.

He stood there for a minute, with just the sound of the wind. A lantern flared in the window behind him, and he saw the shape of Auntie Florence moving around in the kitchen.

He thought about sitting in his Thinking Place, even though it was dark, just to contemplate what had happened. But instead, he put one foot in front of the other and headed for the door.

Auntie Florence was waving a church fan in front of her face, sitting on her *chaise*. "Hey, Auntie," Sacky greeted her.

She looked up and shook her head. "Hot as the devil's breath in this house," she said.

Sacky swallowed hard.

Auntie Florence set down the fan and stood up. She was a tall woman, with nice gray hair she always kept pretty. "Sacky," she started, "I been at church all this time, praising the Lord. Your auntie's too tired to cook now, so how about a little surprise instead?"

Sacky raised his eyebrows. He'd had enough surprises for one night.

"What kind of surprise?" he ventured.

"Some of that yellow cake in the kitchen," his auntie said, "and you can have two whole slices."

Sacky's eyes lit up. "For dinner? Two slices?"

"Yes, child, two. Now, hurry up before I change my mind."

Sacky ran to the kitchen, his mouth already watering, ready to taste the best yellow cake in the county.

The Assist

Linda Sue Park and Anna Dobbin

"Okay, guys, time for fartleks!"

Coach O'Brien always ended practice with fartleks, which Eddie thought was possibly the most ridiculous word in the dictionary.

Definitions of *fartlek* from some of the eighth graders on the Lilac Township Middle School boys' soccer team:

 Eddie: "Basically, we start jogging around the field. When Coach blows his whistle, we sprint. When he blows it again, we jog. When he blows it again, we walk. And it cycles like that: jog, sprint, jog, walk, jog."

 James: "A fartlek is humankind's most cruel invention."

 Ben: "JAMES SAID FART!!!"

 Daniel: "Reeeeal original, Ben. And no, James—fartleks are necessary exercises to keep all you bums in shape."

At the end of a long week, fartleks were especially tough, but Eddie knew it was no use arguing with Coach O'Brien. He got into position at the halfway line, with Ben, his co-captain, beside him, and Daniel and James just behind—their usual places. The rest of the team followed, lining up in twos.

Eddie noticed Noah eagerly elbow his way to the third row, right behind Daniel. Noah was a skinny seventh grader who wore his straight brown hair in a mushroom cut. While Eddie wasn't close friends with him, he liked that Noah always tried hard during practice.

Coach blew his whistle.

"Pasta party at my house on Sunday," Ben said as they rounded the first corner of the field at a brisk jog. "You guys coming?"

"Obviously," Eddie said.

Coach blew his whistle again. Eddie heard James groan as the team took off in a full-speed sprint. The neat columns they had been jogging in broke down as the faster players surged ahead and the slower ones struggled to keep up. His legs and arms pumping hard, Eddie counted under his breath: "One, two, three, four . . ."

Whistle.

Twenty pairs of cleats thumped against the dry ground as the boys slowed to a jog, coming back into their two lines.

"Listen, Ben," James panted. "I can only come to the party if I don't die first. My legs are toast."

Daniel scoffed. "One sprint and you're already complaining? Does someone need a wambulance? Waaaaaaah!" Eddie laughed and glanced over his shoulder. Daniel was rubbing his eyes with his fists, making a sound halfway between an ambulance siren and a baby crying.

Whistle.

They walked. James and Daniel shoved each other.

Whistle. Coach O'Brien never let them walk for long.

"I'm *joking,*" James said as they began to jog again. "The UN never misses a pasta party."

Last year, Coach had started calling Eddie and his friends "the UN" because they were so mixed ethnically: Eddie was half Korean American and half Irish, Daniel was half Jamaican and half African American, James's parents were from Iran, and Ben and his family had immigrated from Italy when he was a little kid. Their passion for soccer bound them together, and they played central positions on the field: striker, center midfielder, sweeper, and goalkeeper.

Soccer positions as written down by Eddie in an effort to impress Mina, a cute girl on the volleyball team:

POSITION	DESCRIPTION	PLAYER
Striker	Very fast, but lazy and cocky. Known for short bursts of high speed, but is otherwise scratching his butt at the halfway line while the rest of the team plays defense.	James

POSITION	DESCRIPTION	PLAYER
Center midfielder	The guy in the middle, equal parts defender and attacker. Fittest person on the team. A smart player, but kind of a control freak (being in the center makes him feel like he's responsible for everybody).	Daniel
Sweeper	The last line of defense before the keeper. Level-headed. Does not panic easily. As fast as a striker but definitely not lazy. Really good-looking.	Eddie
Goalkeeper	Protects the net. Loud. Confident. Not afraid of soccer balls flying at his face (i.e., has an underdeveloped sense of self-preservation).	Ben

Whistle. The boys sprinted.

Eddie kept track of their laps around the field. Coach was predictable: he always made them do three, and always ended on a sprint. As the team rounded the last corner of the third lap, Noah appeared in Eddie's peripheral vision. The seventh grader had begun speeding up in anticipation of Coach's final whistle.

"See you fartlekkers later!" Noah shouted. He blew into the crook of his elbow, making a loud flatulent noise as he motored past.

Whistle.

"Son of a . . . ," James muttered, chasing after Noah. Eddie snickered. The only thing that trumped James's hatred of running drills was his desire not to be outdone by a seventh grader.

James's and Noah's cleats hit the halfway line at the same time. Eddie was a close third. He slowed to a walk and interlaced his fingers behind his head, catching his breath, his quads burning.

"Well done, boys," Coach said as he clapped his hands. "Bring it in."

The team formed a circle.

"It's crucial that we bring our absolute best against Southwood on Monday," Coach said. "I want everyone to take it easy this weekend. Don't do anything stupid and get yourself injured. Do I make myself clear?"

The boys murmured in agreement. They all knew where they stood in the league rankings: to make the playoffs, they had to beat Southwood. If they tied or lost, they'd be out of the running for the playoff trophy.

"All right, then," Coach said. "Hands in."

Everybody piled their hands on top of one another's.

Eddie's and Ben's eyes met, then they counted off together: "One, two, three—" "TEAM!"

In the locker room, Ben reminded everyone about the pasta party on Sunday. Pasta parties usually happened the nights before big games. The team gathered at one player's house, discussed strategy, and ate a crap-ton of spaghetti and meatballs cooked by parent volunteers. Or a grandparent, in Ben's case: his nonna was like one of those stereotypical Italian grannies in marinara-sauce commercials. Pasta nights at Ben's house were generally acknowledged to be the best.

After changing clothes, Eddie left the locker room with Daniel, James, and Ben. They were almost at the front door of the school building when Eddie realized he'd forgotten his phone. He said bye to his friends, then turned around and hurried back.

As he approached the locker room door, he opened his duffel bag and began rummaging around inside it, thinking maybe his phone was just buried somewhere in a week's worth of stinky soccer socks. He pushed the door open with his shoulder—

CRASH!

Eddie collided with Noah, who was walking out right at that moment. Noah fell on his butt, the papers in his hands flying everywhere. Eddie stumbled backward but managed to stay on his feet. The strap of his open duffel slipped off his shoulder, and the bag hit the tile floor, half the contents tumbling out.

"Oh, sorry, man," Eddie said, immediately stepping forward and offering Noah a hand. A little dazed, the younger boy took it, and Eddie hauled him upright. "You okay?"

"Yeah, um, my bad," Noah said. He shook his head as if to clear it, then quickly stooped to collect the papers he'd dropped.

One sheet of paper had ended up on Eddie's stuff. As Eddie grabbed it, his gaze landed on the words at the top:

FreeEnglishEssays.com

SAMPLE ENGLISH LITERATURE ESSAY

Identity and Adversity in *All American Boys*
by Jason Reynolds and Brendan Kiely

"You're reading *All American Boys*?" Eddie asked. "So you're in Mrs. Shankar's class?" He'd had her last year. She always chose good books, which he missed now that Mr. Lawson was his teacher. A nice guy, but he was a million years old and had been teaching the same boring stuff his entire life. Eddie could only read so much Shakespeare before he went as insane as . . . well, pretty much every Shakespeare character ever.

Noah didn't answer. He snatched the paper from Eddie and stuffed it hastily into his backpack. "I gotta go," he mumbled.

"That's a cool book," Eddie said, trying to stall the other boy. Something smelled fishy, and he didn't think it was his soccer socks.

"Yep," said Noah. He took a step to try to walk around Eddie.

Eddie blocked the door. "What's with that essay?"

Noah's eyes darted. "It's nothing."

Eddie raised an eyebrow and waited.

"It's research," Noah said. "I mean, I pulled that from the internet to help me figure out what to write about."

"When's the essay due?"

"Um . . . it was due on Wednesday. Shanks gave me until Monday to turn it in."

"She did?" Eddie remembered that Mrs. Shankar typically didn't accept late work. She was strict like that.

Noah fell silent.

"What's going on, man?" Eddie said.

The seventh grader hesitated. "I begged her," he finally blurted, and then the words started spilling out of his mouth fast. "I suck at English, okay? I actually really liked the book, but I didn't do the essay, because I suck at writing. But then today after class, Shanks told me my grade is a C minus."

Eddie inhaled sharply through his teeth. Everyone on the team knew that they had to maintain at least a C average in each class, or else they wouldn't be allowed to compete in games—school policy for all student-athletes at Lilac Township Middle.

"Yeah," Noah said. "So she said she was going to report my grade to Coach. And then I wouldn't be able to play on Monday. I, like, basically got down on my knees and begged until she let me have an extension."

Nodding, Eddie gave him a sympathetic look. He would have begged, too, in the same situation—not that he would *ever* get a C minus in anything. His parents would skin him alive or, worse, take away his Nintendo 3DS.

Then a realization lit up Eddie's brain. "Hey. You're not going to turn that paper in like it's yours, are you?"

"I *have* to," Noah whispered, even though there was nobody else around. "Shanks is already docking me a full letter grade because I'm turning it in late. So I'm starting with a B. And it has to be good enough to get my overall grade up to a C."

Just then, Eddie heard his ringtone echoing through the room. He was right—he'd left his phone in his locker. It was probably Mom calling from the parking lot, wondering what the heck was taking so long.

Noah reached past Eddie and put his hand on the door, trying to leave again.

Eddie knew it would be easiest to just do nothing—to forget about Noah, go home, eat dinner, and play *Super Smash Bros.* until bed. But if there was one thing he had learned from soccer, it was that doing nothing was actually a choice.

A SOCCER PLAYER'S CHOICES DURING EVERY PLAY OF A GAME:

- Watch the play constantly and anticipate, so you can move into the right position. FAST, when necessary. Which is almost always.

- Make a half-hearted attempt at the above, ending up in position too late.

- Do nothing. Stand still, fuming at the ref's last call or the other team's unfair play—for seconds that could end up being crucial.

"Wait," Eddie said quickly, before Noah could push past him. "I've read the book. I can help you with your essay."

Noah flicked his gaze up to Eddie's face. "I don't need help."

"If you get caught cheating, you won't just be out for the game. You'll get kicked off the team."

Noah's forehead creased with worry.

"And you *will* get caught," Eddie added. "Teachers know how to Google, too."

Eddie's ringtone ended. After a long silence, Noah finally gave a small nod.

"I'll help you draft it tomorrow," Eddie said.

"I can't tomorrow," said Noah. "We're going to visit my aunt this weekend. I won't be home until Sunday afternoon."

"Okay, so, Sunday night."

"But what about the pasta party?"

Eddie sighed, then looked Noah right in the eye. "I guess we're not going."

The pasta party was scheduled to start at six o'clock. Just before six-thirty, Eddie was parking his bike in front of Coffee Cave, where he'd arranged to meet Noah, when his phone buzzed with a text from Ben.

Where u at?

Eddie felt a twinge of guilt. As co-captain, he should have let Ben know that he wouldn't be at the pasta party. But he had put off telling Ben because he figured it wouldn't be cool to blab about Noah's problems.

Something came up.

No way. It's not a PP without the entire UN. Get ur butt over here.

I can't. Tell you later. Sorry to the team and nonna.

Whatever dude. Nonna is shaking her wooden spoon at u.

Eddie grimaced. He knew his co-captain well enough to see through his humor—Ben was pissed off that Eddie wasn't there. Putting his phone back in his pocket, Eddie pushed open the door of the coffee shop.

Noah was already sitting in a corner booth. *Good,* Eddie thought. *One point in the little twerp's favor.* The text exchange with Ben had left him in a sour mood.

"Let's get started," he said brusquely as he sat down opposite Noah. "Show me what you've done so far."

Noah looked alarmed, either at Eddie's words or his tone or both. "Um. I don't—I mean, isn't that why we're doing this?" He turned his laptop around so Eddie could see the screen.

There was nothing on it except Noah's name and the date.

Eddie felt his anger rising. *I should be at the pasta party, with the rest of the team. I have a responsibility to them, too, and this guy didn't even care enough to try—*

"I tried to start it," Noah said. He sounded really miserable. "About a hundred times. I just can't—I can never think of anything to write."

Eddie was quiet for a moment. *Okay, so I'd rather be somewhere else. But we're here now. Might as well do this.*

"Get out your phone," he said. "I'm gonna text you some questions, and you text me back the answers, okay?"

Noah seemed baffled, but he grabbed his phone from his backpack.

> Who's your favorite character?

Rashad

> What do you like about him?

Well he's the hero of the story, right?

> Not what I meant. What happens in the story that makes you like him?

Oh. He seems really real. Like he's scared when the cop has him down on the ground. I would be too. And he gets confused by his brother and his dad.

"Okay," Eddie said. "Switch to the laptop now. Look at your phone, and start typing out what you just texted me. But in better sentences."

He was showing Noah a trick he had learned from his aunt Margaret, his dad's sister. She taught writing at a nearby community college and loved using technology to help people write better.

"Really?" Noah looked surprised.

"Yeah, really."

"Like this?" As Noah typed, he said the words aloud. "In . . . *All American* . . . *Boys*"—he paused to look at his phone—"Rashad . . . is my . . . favorite . . . character."

"Good. Add the author's name."

"Two authors," Noah pointed out.

"Right. Now, when you do the transfer from your phone to the laptop, make it sound more English-y. Like, 'really real' doesn't sound like an essay—know what I mean?"

"So what should I say instead?"

"Come on, man. I'm not writing it for you. Just try to say it a different way."

Fifteen minutes later, Noah had written three complete sentences:

> In *All American Boys* by Brendan Kiely and Jason Reynolds, Rashad is my favorite character. He seems very realistic in his emotions. For example, he's afraid when the cop pins him down on the ground.

"The next part's easy," Eddie said. "Find that place in the book, the scene with the cop, and cite it. Not too much, but up to, like, three or four sentences. Copy it word for word, with quotation marks, and then put the page number in parentheses."

Noah did as instructed. When he was done, he grinned at the screen, and then at Eddie.

"That makes it longer without having to think of what to write," he gloated.

"Yeah, but you should only do it a few times. Most of the essay is supposed to be *your* words."

More essay tips, presented by the members of the UN:

Eddie: "Just start writing. Starting is the hardest part."

James: "Wait until you get that lightning bolt of inspiration. For me, that usually happens a few hours before the essay is due."

Ben: "Probably my best advice is to never listen to James under any circumstances."

Daniel: "Seconded."

James: "Here's a tip, guys: Go run a fartlek off a cliff."

The session continued, a paragraph at a time: Eddie texting questions, Noah texting back his answers and then transferring those responses to the laptop, revising and editing as he went. After the fourth paragraph, Noah looked much less tense.

"I think I'm getting the hang of this," he said. "When I text you, it's like I'm just talking about a book I liked."

"It's always easier when you like the book," Eddie agreed. "My aunt Margaret says a lot of people are scared of writing, but no one's scared of texting. The texting helps you figure out what to say, and then when you transfer it to the laptop, you figure out how to say it."

Despite Noah's newfound enthusiasm, it still took almost three hours for him to write the whole essay. Eddie continued to text questions for each paragraph, and then gave him pointers on how to improve the work. By the time Noah was finished, both boys were exhausted.

As they packed up their things, Eddie gave Noah a tip for the next essay: take screenshots of their text exchange and use the same questions again. "You might have to sort of adapt them," Eddie said, "but most of what I asked you can apply to any book."

"Thanks," Noah said. Then, hesitantly: "Do you think this will get a good enough grade?"

Eddie wasn't sure what to say. He wanted to be both encouraging and realistic, a tricky combination.

"I hope so," he said. "And you gotta look at it this way: no matter what grade you get, it's better than cheating."

"Nah," Noah said. "Cheating would have been a lot easier."

"*What*—" Eddie started to say, in outrage and disappointment.

But then Noah pointed at him. "Gotcha," he said with a smirk.

Eddie rolled his eyes. "Go home and go to bed. This is your captain speaking."

It was game day. Qualify-for-the-playoffs day. We-can't-mess-this-up day.

Eddie saw Noah in the hallway after school. Even before asking, he knew from Noah's glum face that it wasn't good news.

"C," Noah said. "That means it was a B, which is the best I ever did on an essay. But it was lowered a whole grade for being late, so my average is still a C minus."

"Sorry, man," Eddie said.

"I just saw Shanks go into Coach's office," Noah said. "So, yeah, I'm screwed. Crush Southwood today, okay?"

As Noah walked away, Eddie was surprised at how he felt. He hadn't expected to be so upset. But it was as if he had let Noah and himself and the whole team down.

Eddie headed for the locker room, silently vowing to play his absolute hardest.

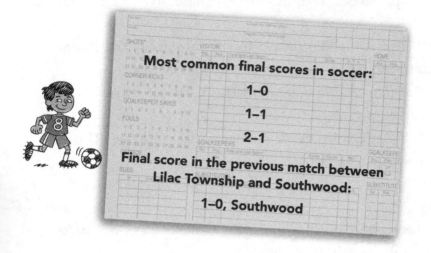

Most common final scores in soccer:

1–0

1–1

2–1

Final score in the previous match between Lilac Township and Southwood:

1–0, Southwood

At halftime, the score was still 0–0.

It was a cold afternoon, the temperature in the forties. As the Lilac offense set up a corner kick early in the second half, Eddie glanced at the sidelines. Behind Coach were eight boys on the bench, waiting for their turn to sub in, their legs bouncing to keep warm.

There should have been nine boys, but a certain seventh grader was missing. A fresh wave of disappointment washed over Eddie, right there on the field.

Hearing shouts, Eddie snapped his attention back to the game. The corner kick was arcing toward the goal. James leaped up for the header, but the Southwood keeper stepped in front of him and snatched the ball out of the air.

That was as close as they got to Southwood's goal for almost twenty minutes. Their defense was like a wall.

Southwood's offense began pressing harder as the clock ran down. With five minutes to go, the ball popped out from a frantic knot of players in front of Lilac's goal, and Daniel managed to clear it. Then, at last, James picked it up at midfield, turned, and took off.

Breakaway!

"Move up!" Ben screamed from the net. "MOVE UP! PUT THE PRESSURE ON!"

The Lilac defense complied, jogging forward. Eddie squinted against the harsh wind, his eyes on James.

There were only two defenders between James and the Southwood goalie. James juked around one with a quick, fluid move (which he would talk about for days afterward) and picked up speed again.

"Come on!" Eddie shouted.

James could have been all alone on the field—that was how fast he was running. Only one more player to beat . . .

BAM! Southwood's sweeper came in with a hard slide tackle that cut James's feet out from under him. He fell forward, crashed onto his hands and knees, and immediately rolled over, grabbing his left ankle.

The referee whistled for an injury time-out.

James was groaning when Eddie reached him. With his face contorted, he muttered some very expressive phrases. It looked like he had taken the brunt of the tackle on his left instep, where his foot met his ankle—a spot unprotected by his shin guard.

"I'm fine," James said. But when he tried to stand, he crumpled to the ground again, repeating those colorful phrases.

By this time, Coach had run over. He squatted down and prodded James's foot gently. James yelped, and Eddie saw him close his eyes tightly against tears.

Daniel hoisted James to his feet and helped him limp off the field. Ms. Morris, the assistant coach and team trainer, hurried to meet them with the first aid kit. The rest of the team dispersed to their positions or to the sidelines.

"Sub, ref!" Coach said, then turned toward the bench. "Noah! You're in!"

Eddie's mouth fell open.

Noah?

There was no time to ask questions. The whistle blew, and the game restarted.

Within fifteen seconds, two Southwood forwards were bearing down on Eddie. They passed around him, a classic give-and-go, then *boom*—a hard shot sailed toward the Lilac net.

Time slowed. Eddie could've sworn his heart stopped beating for a second.

Ben dove—a spectacular dive—and grabbed the ball. He curled his body over it, despite what seemed like a dozen Southwood cleats pummeling it. Then he scrambled to his feet and hurled the ball sidearm, straight to Eddie.

He trapped the ball. Looked up. Saw Noah, his skinny legs propelling him down the field.

Eddie didn't think; he just reacted.

"NOAH!" he bellowed, then kicked the ball as hard as he could.

In one of those never-to-be-repeated miracles, the ball soared in an arc overhead, then descended to meet the foot of the sprinting Noah, as if some invisible soccer spirit had placed it there. Noah took two steps—one dribble—which put him just inside the penalty box. He drew back his right foot . . . waited a split second, until Southwood's goalie leaned right . . . then rocketed the ball into the upper left corner of the net.

1–0, Lilac.

The game-ending whistle blew thirty seconds later, and the Lilac Township side erupted in cheers.

It was pandemonium. Noah was hoisted onto his teammates' shoulders and carried aloft in front of the happy, half-frozen fans in the bleachers. Ben's head got thoroughly noogied for that crucial late save. James's efforts were lauded, too. "Did you *see* that move right before I went down?" he kept saying.

"No, we didn't," Daniel said, rolling his eyes. "*Please* tell us about it again."

Eddie sat down on the bleachers, a short distance from the commotion. His legs needed a rest—he'd played nearly the whole match. He saw Noah break free from the celebrating crowd and jog toward him.

Eddie called out as Noah drew nearer. "That shot should be on ESPN."

"Well, I don't know if you noticed, but there was this amazing assist that set it up," Noah said, beaming.

"Why did you get to play? You said—"

"Shanks worked it out with Coach," Noah cut in. "She told him that my essay was a big improvement over what I've been handing in. So they made a deal: if I turn in an extra-credit assignment this week, I could play."

He explained that Coach had called him while the team was warming up and told him about the arrangement with Mrs. Shankar. Noah had already taken the bus home, and his mom had been stuck at work—but she'd managed to get him to the field during the second half. Absorbed in the game, Eddie hadn't noticed him arrive.

"Anyway," Noah said, glancing at his feet, suddenly shy. "Thanks for your help."

"Thanks for getting us into the playoffs," Eddie replied.

"Yo!"

They looked toward the voice. The other players were lining up for a team photo, and Ben's goalie-gloved hands were cupped around his mouth. "Hurry up!" he shouted. "I'm freezing my fartleks off!"

Laughing, Eddie stood, and he and Noah began walking toward the group.

"So what are you going to do for extra credit?" Eddie asked.

"I'm not sure yet," Noah said, smiling. "I'll text you."

The UN's favorite emojis:

Eddie: ⚽

James: 💪

Ben: 💩

Daniel: 🙄

Noah: 😂

Home

Hena Khan

A blast of heat hits my face as I walk out of our hotel into the fierce sunlight. Luckily, there's an air-conditioned taxi parked in front of the building, and I hop inside with my parents. Baba asks the driver in broken Arabic to take us to the hospital. He says *hospital,* but he means the orphanage on the fifth floor of the hospital building in Meknes. We're visiting this city in Morocco during the hottest month of the summer.

When my mom went with a friend to visit the orphanage last year, I imagined it was like the one in the movie *Annie*. Back home in Virginia, Mama told me it wasn't anything like that. There was no mean Miss Hannigan, no singing and dancing, and a lot more boys than girls. One of them is my new little brother, Hakeem, who I'm about to meet for the first time.

We arrive at the square gray building and there's no elevator to get to the fifth floor. For the next ten minutes, all we hear is the slap of our shoes against endless stone steps and our own heavy breathing in the sweltering stairwell.

"Two more," Mama pants as we get to floor three. Her face is red.

"At least we got a workout in today, right, Aleena?" Baba says to me. I'm too hot to smile at him. I'm carrying the raccoon backpack I brought for Hakeem, and wearing my matching penguin one. Sweat is dripping down the back of my neck.

Finally we reach the top floor and my heart is hammering in my chest. It's only partly because of the heat and the stairs. Mostly it's because I'm finally going to see Hakeem in real life. This is the moment I've been waiting for since last year, ever since my parents asked my older brother, Bilal, and me if we would "welcome a three-year-old boy into our family." I screamed yes and jumped up and down.

It was an easy decision. I felt like I already knew Hakeem. We'd been getting photos and videos of this curly-haired kid with shiny brown eyes after my mom's first visit. Our family started sponsoring Hakeem to go to preschool. Mama wanted to do something to help the orphans she saw, and that was supposed to be it. But the more time that went by, with every update we got, we all thought about Hakeem more and more. And each of us felt that he belonged in our family.

Now I'm bringing him home with my parents, without my older brother. Bilal has summer training with his soccer team and can't miss the first four days of his sophomore year of high school. I'm supposed to be starting middle school next week, and will have to wait until I'm back to find out where my locker is and get my schedule. But I wouldn't trade being here for anything.

A lady with a smiling face and a blue hijab greets us with lots of nodding, and ushers us into a room that has built-in bench sofas with a busy pattern on the fabric. Another family is already inside with a toddler, who's playing with a small red soccer ball.

"This is it," Mama says as she squeezes my hand. "Are you ready?"

"*Naam*." I practice my Arabic for "yes." I've been writing down words and phrases like *"kan bgreek,"* which means "I love you," into a tiny notebook since Hakeem doesn't speak English and we don't speak Arabic. I don't realize I'm nervously tapping my leg against the bench until the other kid suddenly stops playing to stare at me.

"Remember," Mama says to me. "We can't take Hakeem with us today. We have to wait for his paperwork and passport. And that could take two weeks."

"I know," I reply, although it's going to be so hard to leave for the hotel without him.

The door opens and in walks the blue hijab lady with a little boy clutching her hand. It's Hakeem. He seems smaller than in his pictures, but is just as adorable. We've been sending photos and videos of ourselves, so he should be able to recognize us.

Hakeem doesn't move at first as he scans the room. Then he suddenly lights up as he looks at me. I smile and open my arms for a hug. He runs toward me . . .

And runs right past me and over to . . . the red ball! The other kid grabs it before Hakeem can pick it up.

"Hakeem, here," I quickly say, holding out the backpack I brought him. I unzip it and show him the stuffed dog toy that I sprayed with Mama's perfume inside.

Hakeem glances at me for a split second, before turning back to the boy and the ball. The ball bounces on the floor and Hakeem watches it until it stops. He picks it up and throws it and watches it bounce again. It's like we aren't even in the room.

"Mama, what is he doing?" I whisper, although I know he can't understand what I'm saying. "Why isn't he coming to us?"

"It's okay, love. I don't think he's seen a ball before." Mama settles into the bench and smiles. She doesn't seem to mind that she just traveled across the world from America to finally be with her son, and that he hasn't noticed her. But she doesn't take her eyes off Hakeem for a second.

✦ ✦ ✦

"Aren't you happy to see Hakeem again?" Baba searches my face on our way to the orphanage the next day.

"Yeah, but I don't think he likes me," I say, thinking about how he was more excited about a ball than meeting me.

"I'm sure it's not that," Baba says. "It's all overwhelming for him. He's just overstimulated."

Overstimulated. That's the understatement of the year. It turns out my new brother can't sit still every time we visit him. The *Cars* crayon set and coloring book I bring him? They entertain him for about two minutes. The Elmo puzzle? He doesn't understand what to do with it and throws the pieces all over the place while I try to show him.

But every day Hakeem wears the backpack I brought him when he comes into the room for our visits. He looks at us with a face filled with a mixture of joy and shyness. As each day goes by, he sits in my parents' laps longer, hugs me harder, and repeats *"kan bgreek"* when it's time for him to return to his room. I say "I love you" to him, too, so he can start to learn English.

We get to see his room one day when we go on a tour of the rest of the orphanage. The blue hijab lady who I now know is named Sister Khalida first takes us to the space for babies, filled with rows and rows of metal cribs. A couple of babies are crying, and the rest are sleeping or just lying there.

Sister Khalida stops in the middle of the room and points to a crib over and over again.

"That must be where Hakeem slept until he was two years old," Mama says, wiping her eyes. I imagine a tinier version of him lying here with no mother or father to love him, and my eyes fill up, too.

Next we go into the room for kids who are older than two, like Hakeem. The kids aren't there, and I'm a little relieved. It's hard enough to see the rows of cots, arranged like the cribs, only larger. It makes my insides twist into knots.

"They have food and clothing and a place to sleep here," Mama says aloud to no one in particular as she blows her nose. "But no playgrounds, no bath toys, no cuddle times for these kids. It's heartbreaking."

"Can't we take all of them?" I suddenly blurt out. I haven't said a word since we started the tour. "Maybe Mariya Auntie can adopt one, and Mrs. Jenkins always says how much she loves kids. . . ."

"It's not that simple," Mama sighs. "We're blessed to get to take Hakeem home, and so quickly."

It's almost been a year since we first talked about it, so it doesn't feel quick at all. I can't wait to get him out of this place.

✦ ✦ ✦

"Mama!" I yell. "Hakeem messed up my room again!"

I just got back from school, and it's like a burglar came in, searched for things to steal, and left it a complete disaster.

"It's okay," Mama calls from downstairs. "I'll help you clean up."

I sit on my bed and look around my room, which is a blur through my angry tears. Before Hakeem came home with us a month ago, it was perfect. The walls were painted exactly like I wanted: pink and gold. Now there are ugly marker scribbles that Hakeem drew everywhere that won't wash off. Baba promised to paint over them more than a week ago, but he still hasn't done it.

Mama rushes in.

"It's not so bad," she sighs as she surveys my books dumped out of the bookshelves, my hamper knocked over, and all my Legos creations smashed into pieces.

"It's not *your* room." I sniffle. "Why is he always in here? Why can't I get a lock on my door?"

"We are not going to lock your brother out of any part of the house. He has to learn."

He has to learn. That's the new understatement of the year. Hakeem gets a pass for everything bad he does because he doesn't understand English, or because he's never seen books or Legos before. I've been teaching him so many things every single day, but sometimes it feels like he hasn't learned anything since he left the orphanage weeks ago.

Before I can stop them, images of the orphanage fill my mind. I picture Hakeem's cot, and all the kids who we left behind, like Hakeem's best friend. I remember him crying when Hakeem said goodbye. And I start to feel guilty for a second . . .

Until I spot the slime.

"Ahhhhhh!" I wail. "Look!"

Right in front of my closet, all my ziplock bags of colorful scented slime are open and have oozed onto my cream-colored carpet.

"Oh no." Mama frowns. "This is bad."

"I know!" I start to cry. "This was my best batch of slime! It's sugar cookie and pumpkin flavor. And I used all my glitter in it!"

"You shouldn't have left it within Hakeem's reach," Mama scolds as she examines the damage to the carpet.

"So it's *my fault*?" I know I shouldn't be yelling, but I can't help it. I already got into big trouble when Hakeem cut his own hair, along with my favorite doll's, for leaving scissors "within his reach." He seems to be able to reach anything and find everything, no matter where I hide it.

"Stop shouting. You can always make more slime. This carpet is another story. Did you have to dye this stuff pink and orange?"

"All you care about is the carpet. And *his* feelings," I mutter.

It's exactly the same way with my dad and Bilal. They always take Hakeem's side and say I'm being mean or sensitive when I get upset with him. It's not fair, because it's always my stuff he messes up, not theirs. And isn't it a good thing to be "sensitive," anyway?

Hakeem sticks his head inside the door, smiles his most charming smile, and points at me. That's usually enough to make me smile back and forgive him. But not today.

"Get *out!*" I jump up and slam the door shut. While the door closes, I see Hakeem's eyes grow bigger as he steps backward, out of the way.

My parents like to remind me of the day I said yes to adopting him whenever I complain about Hakeem ruining my life. What did I know when I wasn't even eleven years old yet? Starting middle school has been hard enough, without having my whole world—and my room—turned upside down.

I ignore Hakeem for the rest of the day. When he makes funny faces, whispers "Leeeeeena," and tries to get me to laugh during dinner, I look away.

As we pull up to the soccer field, Bilal comes running to the minivan in his training jersey.

"Can I take Hakeem to meet the team?" he asks, sticking his head through the window.

"Now? I need to get back by six for a conference call," Mama says. "And Hakeem got up early today and didn't nap. He's really tired."

Mama yawns as she says the last words and I can tell she's tired, too. She'll never admit that Hakeem is wearing her out. The rest of us get a break during the day when we're at school or work, but Mama works from home. And I overheard her last week complaining to Baba that she can't get anything done and needs time to herself.

"I'll be quick. Come on, Hakeem, the guys want to meet you."

"Guys," Hakeem repeats. He's turned into a parrot the past few days, repeating everything we say. It's kind of cute, but I'm still mad at him. It's been three days since the slime incident, and my carpet has a gigantic stain that we can't scrub out. Between that and the marker on the walls, my room is a total wreck.

"Yes, we're going to see the guys." Bilal picks Hakeem out of his booster seat and starts to walk away. Then he turns back.

"Come on, Aleena."

I scramble out of the car behind them. Bilal's team is always psyched to see me, especially if I'm in my soccer uniform. I love it when they call me Little A and let me kick the ball around with them.

"There he is!" Bilal's best friend, David, is beaming as we approach. "Hey, big guy. You know how to kick a ball?"

"Ball!" Hakeem says, and David and the rest of the team laugh at his accent.

The next thing I know, Hakeem is running all over the field and the whole team is cheering for him. I've been showing him how to kick the ball around in the backyard, and it's pretty amazing to see how good he is now, especially since a month ago he didn't know what a ball was.

"Bee-*laal*!" Hakeem says *Bilal* the way they do in Arabic and everyone starts chanting, "Bee-*laal*."

I stand on the sideline, feeling invisible. The guys don't even notice I'm here. After a couple of minutes, I walk back to the car to wait with Mama.

"Are they coming?" Mama asks.

"I don't know," I grumble.

"Well, what are they doing?"

"Playing soccer."

"Didn't I tell Bilal I have to get home? Can you please go get them?"

I'm deciding whether to protest or just get out of the car again when I see Bilal and David walking to the parking lot. David is carrying Hakeem and when they get to the car, Hakeem gives David a high five.

As he is about to walk away, David turns back and says, "Hi, Mrs. S. Hey, Little A! Next time we need you to play, too, okay?"

I nod as Hakeem mimics him and says "Little A!" Everyone laughs. And though I don't want to, the silly way he says it and peers at me with his eyebrows raised makes me smile a little.

"Let's go home," Mama says.

"Home?" Hakeem asks, turning to me. I'm the one he always turns to when he doesn't understand something.

"I'll show you what it is when we get there," I promise with a sigh. When we pull into the driveway, I remember to point it out.

"*Home,* Hakeem," I say as I motion toward the house. "This is home."

At bedtime, I hear Hakeem and Mama in his room. For the past week, before getting tucked in, Hakeem has been pointing at his wall with the airplane decals, his bucket of cars, his comforter, and his other stuff and saying "Thank you" to each of them. He just started doing it one day, and now it's kind of his thing. Tonight, when he's done, I hear him pause and then add, "Thank you, home."

"Can you make sure he doesn't bother us?"

I've planned out everything about my art-themed twelfth birthday party over the past three weeks. We're going to do two craft projects in the backyard. With eight girls coming over, the last thing I want is for Hakeem to be hyper and get in the way.

"Yes." Mama exhales slowly. "I'll keep him inside, okay?"

The goody bags for my friends are laid out on the patio table. I decorated each bag and filled them with mini watercolor sets and notepads and my favorite candy. Mama and I made cupcakes last night and hid them on the highest shelf of the refrigerator, and I picked out candles from the party store that look like crayons.

"You're lucky it's a beautiful day. No rain in the forecast," Baba says as he ties pink and gold balloons to the mailbox. Of course Baba has to give a balloon to Hakeem, and he runs around the yard, batting it into the air. I hope it tires him out enough that he'll be happy to stay inside and watch a movie while my friends are here.

As everyone starts to arrive, Hakeem is surprisingly calm. Maybe he's acting shy because there are so many girls, but he stands behind Mama and peeks out at them.

"He's so cute," Priscilla says with a little wave. "Hi, Hakeem!"

"Don't talk to him," I warn. "He'll want all your attention and you'll have to high-five him fifty times. Let's go in the backyard."

As we walk back there, everything looks perfect. Bilal set up his speakers, and as they fill the air with the sounds of jazz, I feel extra grown up while we work on a sand art project first. I carefully fill a bottle with layers of different-colored sand and top it with a cork. Everyone's looks great, but Keisha is so meticulous with the funnel that her finished bottle looks professional.

"You're so good at that!" Sabriya admires Keisha's handiwork as we move on to paint mugs next.

I decide I'm going to paint my mug for my mom, since Hakeem broke the handle of her favorite one last week. I make a big heart in the middle and fill it in with smaller hearts.

"Are you girls thirsty?" Mama comes outside carrying pink lemonade and some cups. We take a break from painting and sit in the grass under the tree in the shade, sipping our drinks and talking.

"How about cake in half an hour?" Mama asks.

"Sure, thank you, Mrs. Siddiqui," the girls say in a chorus. I smile at Mama and she winks as she heads back toward the sliding door to the kitchen. Everything is going perfectly so far, exactly as I imagined it. And Hakeem has been staying out of sight and out of trouble.

"I'm going to ask my parents if I can have a party like this," Priscilla says. "It's such a good idea."

"Me too," adds Sabriya.

"Thanks," I say.

Keisha starts to tell us a story about her teacher at school who adopted a shelter dog and then had a horrible allergic reaction and now is looking for a new owner. We're all talking about how we wish we could help, when I hear Hakeem's voice.

"Leeeeena! Play?"

I turn around and see Hakeem beckoning me from be-hind Izzy.

"You're supposed to be inside," I say. "Go back."

Hakeem shakes his head and waves his fingers at me like he's casting a spell. That's when I notice that they are covered with sand. Multicolored sand. *Wait a—*

"Mama!" I yell as I run to the sand art station. Sure enough, it is destroyed. Hakeem dumped out every single one of the little bottles into an empty flowerpot and made his own sandbox.

"What did you do?" I cry as my friends catch up to me.

"I can't believe this!" someone says as we scan the damage.

"What a monster!" Priscilla declares. "You were right!"

"I thought my sister was bad. But she's never done any-thing like this!" Sabriya adds.

"You ruined all our work!" Keisha accuses Hakeem, and I see him shrink from the harshness of her words. Part of me is glad. He deserves it.

Mama and Baba come running outside.

"I thought he was inside with Bilal!" Mama says. "We were getting the food ready!"

I stare angrily at Hakeem. There isn't enough new sand left to refill the bottles.

"Leena . . . ," he starts to say. But then his face crumples and he runs to Mama and hides it. I've only ever seen him cry twice before—when he said goodbye to the kids at the orphanage and one night at home when he first arrived. And now this.

"I'm sorry, hon," Mama says to me. "Don't let this ruin the party, okay? I'm bringing the food out in a moment. Hakeem, you come with me, mister. You're staying inside for the rest of the time."

Hakeem follows my parents into the house. There are tears on his face, and sand all over his shoes, leaving a trail behind him on the patio.

"I'm *so* glad I don't have a little brother," Izzy declares.

"But I wanted one so much," I remember. "And I was so happy when we got him."

"Yeah, until he ruined your stuff and trashed your room," Carmen adds. "I would be so mad." I don't even remember telling my friends about that. Baba finally painted over Hakeem's scribbles on the walls last weekend, and I can barely see it anymore. A steam cleaning made the carpet stain a lot lighter, too. It finally feels like my room again, and Hakeem hasn't done anything else to it this week.

"No wonder you don't want us to come over here most of the time." Keisha sighs. "I don't blame you."

"Me either," Priscilla agrees. "He's so annoying."

I know my friends are trying to make me feel better, but it isn't working. Instead, their words swirl inside me and make me feel emptier than the bottles without any sand left in them.

"No, you guys. You shouldn't say those things," I finally respond. "Hakeem's learning. He didn't have anything in his orphanage, and gets overstimulated. He just wanted to play with the sand. We can put it back in the bottles even if it's mixed up, and maybe add glitter or beads to it to make it pretty."

I look at my friends and wait for their reaction.

"Okay." Keisha shrugs.

"He *is* really cute," Priscilla concedes.

Mama brings out the cupcakes, arranged in a tower. Each one has a candle on it. Baba comes behind her, carrying a fruit platter. And Bilal trails behind with plates and forks.

"You guys ready to sing?" Mama asks cheerfully. Bilal pulls his phone out to take photos.

I glance around for Hakeem and see him standing alone inside the kitchen, his face pressed against the glass of the sliding door.

"Hold on." I stop everyone.

I walk to the door and open it. Hakeem lights up and grabs my hand and practically dances outside.

"Now I'm ready," I say.

I watch as everyone sings to me, including Hakeem, although he's making up his own words. Hakeem's birthday is next month. Or at least we think it is, based on the orphanage paperwork. Mama said it's hard to be sure that it's correct since no one can confirm it. I decide that Hakeem needs to practice before he turns five, so after I blow out my candles, I ask Baba to light them again, and Hakeem takes a turn.

He's so excited that he almost touches a candle, then sticks his finger in a cupcake, licks off the icing, and spits while he blows. We all cheer for him, and he beams and gives everyone high fives.

I suddenly remember my birthday wish from last year, back when we were talking about bringing Hakeem to live with us and be part of our family. It came true. Even though it's been messy sometimes, Hakeem is finally home—and I'm the one who got to teach him what that means.

Ellison's CORNucopia

A LOGAN COUNTY STORY

Lamar Giles

Every Saturday, from nine in the morning to one in the afternoon, the Logan County Farmers' Market opened under a pavilion in the town of Fry, Virginia, rain or shine. This day was a "shine" day with squint-and-shield-your-eyes kind of sun, no clouds, and a sweet, cool breeze blowing. The pavilion, a tent without walls, half the length of a football field, churned with vendors from all over, selling all sorts of things. Mrs. Honeydew had honey from her beloved honeybees, four dollars a jar. Mr. and Mrs. Yeasterly had fresh bread and pastries that were like advertisements for the bakery they were opening soon. The Pepperling family's table was crowded with the plumpest orange and green and red and yellow vegetables, as bright as candy. Then there were the twins, Leen and Vicki "Wiki" Ellison. Two little brown girls who, well . . . sold robots.

Not everyone knew that, of course. Not City Folk, who drove a long way to buy homemade soaps, or fresh pies for dinner parties. Or even Leen and Wiki's uncle Percy, who drove the family's rusted orange pickup truck filled mostly with baskets of corn, and jugs of corn oil, and corn kernels for popping, and corn bread each week. As far as he knew, their family was "so corny!"

(He never failed to tell that joke, or be the only one to laugh at it.)

Though Ellison's CORNucopia did fine business with Logan County's corn lovers, it did not serve the more *specialized* needs of the community. While Uncle Percy napped in the truck—he *always* napped in the truck—Leen and Wiki did business with their *other* regulars.

"I'm going to need five ears, girls. Your corn with some leftover buttered rolls just sounds heavenly," said Miss Wavers, a sweet old lady in big glasses with thick magnifying lenses who was Uncle Percy's third-grade teacher back in the Stone Age. "I'll also need two of those tiny Spider-Rovers, the ones I can control with that special headset."

Leen, always eager to show off her inventions and overly pleased by repeat customers, popped the lid on a fake corn basket and freed two palm-sized metal spiders from their chargers. "Absolutely. My new ones have upgrades you might enjoy. They're lighter and faster, and have a longer battery life."

She stuffed the rovers in a canvas shopping bag with

the corn and quoted Miss Wavers a price. While the lady rummaged in her purse, Wiki said, "Are you having any problems with your old ones?"

"Oh no." She handed over the money. "My other one is so helpful with little chores around the house. I just wanted more."

"Three," Wiki said. "You mean your other three."

Miss Wavers blinked rapidly, realizing her mistake. "Oh yes. Three. How did I forget that?"

Wiki Ellison didn't know how to answer the question, because she didn't forget anything. Ever.

Leen handed Miss Wavers her change. "Thanks for shopping Ellison's CORNucopia! We'll be 'ear' next week!"

Miss Wavers grinned. "So cute."

"Do you have to say that after every sale?" Wiki rolled her eyes and watched Miss Wavers fade into the crowd.

"Uncle Percy said it's like our, uh . . ." Leen couldn't remember the word. Unlike her sister, she often forgot stuff.

"Slogan. I know that, but it's so . . ." She almost said *corny* but caught herself, and let the whole hopeless thing drop. Leen was a stickler for direction, and there was no use arguing. Instead, Wiki settled into her habit of undoing and redoing the elastic tie on her ponytail while observing the thousands of shifting details of this week's farmers' market—details she'd be able to recall a second, minute, month, or year from now with no effort.

Mr. Hannamaker was set up across the main aisle,

three tables down from the CORNucopia, and had on the same shirt he'd worn three Saturdays in a row. Wiki had overheard him tell a customer that he bought a bunch of the same shirts and pants because that's what genius inventor Nikola Tesla—one of Leen's idols—did. Mr. Hannamaker probably meant Albert Einstein, as that was the only genius Wiki had ever read about who kept several versions of the same outfit. Other famous folks who did it were Steve Jobs, and Johnny Cash, and Grace Coddington, and Jerry Garcia, and . . .

"Wiki!" Leen snapped her fingers an inch from her sister's nose, startling her. "You're glitching again."

Wiki plugged her ponytail back through the elastic tie, calculating how long she'd gotten lost in her own head, perhaps ten seconds. It was a sucky side effect of her perfect memory. Sometimes when she recalled things, she thought about other *related* things, then other things on top of that, until she went into a daze, only thinking of things she remembered instead of what was happening in the real world. *Glitching.*

"What was it this time?" Leen asked.

"Mr. Hannamaker's shirt. He's telling people he's got a bunch of the same kind, but it's actually the same shirt. There's a faded mustard stain just over his heart, and a small moth hole two inches below his left shoulder. Both have been there all month."

"So?"

"His potato crop must've been bad this year. He's using thirty percent less table space than he was last season, and he lowered his prices. His truck has a whining fan belt and squeaky brakes. He's also got a bad toothache; he's been poking at it with his tongue all morning, and chewing aspirin every half hour. Those are things people would fix if they had the money. Also . . ." Wiki stopped, reading Leen's face. "I'm not being creepy."

"It's not right, patting other people's pockets. That's what Uncle Percy says."

"I can't help that I notice things, Leen."

"You could try noticing *different* things."

If only it were that easy. Try as she might, odd details jumped at Wiki, like when stuff explodes in those 3-D superhero movies. Even if she looked away, the memory stuck. Still, she pulled her focus from Mr. Hannamaker's table to the one next to his, the Pepperlings' veggie shop. There, another detail jumped.

It was one so obvious Leen noticed it, too. "Hey, what's wrong with Wendy?"

"I don't know."

Wendy Pepperling went to school with the girls, and when Wiki last focused on the Pepperling table, she'd been her usual smiley self. A healthy crowd of shoppers selected cucumbers, and squash, and bulging yellow onions, while

Wendy took money and counted change. Now she was in tears, whipping about frantically behind her table, looking for—

Wiki understood. Her memory of previous observations overlapped with how the Pepperling table looked now, clueing her in to what had happened. One eggplant was gone, purchased by a City Person with a beard and his hair pulled into a tight bun. There were two missing bunches of carrots, purchased by Fry's veterinarian, Dr. Medina, presumably for some animal in her care. A cabbage was gone, and some celery. None of that was unusual, and it certainly wouldn't have made Wendy cry. It was the other missing item, present one hour ago, gone now.

Wiki told Leen, "Someone stole her cashbox."

Leen, admittedly, did not have her sister's attention to detail, unless it was about her inventions. But even she understood how messed up it was for someone to steal Wendy Pepperling's money. So many people here at the farmers' market needed every dollar they made. Uncle Percy was always saying, "The market is how a lot of Logan County stays afloat."

Of course, whenever he said that, she'd start thinking about flotation devices, and how to improve them. She had at least three different hovercraft designs drawn up at—

Oh. Wiki was staring. Now who was glitching?

Wiki shook her head and sucked her teeth. "Watch the table. I'm going to investigate."

"Hey, maybe I want to hear what happened!"

"If someone is stealing cashboxes, then one of us has to stay here, or we gotta carry ours around with us. Uncle Percy would love that!"

Leen smirked. "There is a third option."

Wiki had a computer brain but didn't always problem-solve so well. No worries. That's what sisters were for.

Uncapping the fake corn basket, Leen freed one of her Spider-Rovers. This one had a big green Mountain Dew logo on his back because his hull was built from old soda cans. She called him Dewey. Also, she grabbed her Aug-mented Reality rig from inside the basket—a device that looked kind of like sunglasses, but with only one, clear lens over the right eye. Leen put it on and synced it to Dewey. The rover waggled all eight of his legs before hop-ping upright in Leen's palm. "Lift your shirt. I'm going to put Dewey under it."

Wiki stepped back. "You most certainly will not."

"Dewey has tiny eyes and ears. If you take him with you, then I can see and hear, too."

"Under my shirt, though?"

"Do you really want City Folk to see a metal spider rid-ing on your shoulder? They already think we're weird." Leen frowned. "Until they need corn bread."

No, Wiki didn't want City Folk knowing about their

robot business, and she remembered reading articles about how people trusted you less if you had a camera. A camera inside a robot spider probably made them trust you *a lot* less. She didn't want to frighten Wendy.

Wiki stretched her shirttail toward her sister. "Fine. Just hurry."

Leen shifted her eye slightly, and her headset sent a command to Dewey. The little rover leaped from Leen's palm to Wiki's jeans, then skittered beneath her shirt, forcing the girl to grimace and chuckle at the same time. "It tickles."

At first, all Leen's headset registered was the dark fibers from inside Wiki's clothes, but Dewey made his way to her torso, where his lenses peeked over the shirt collar, giving Leen a view of everything in Wiki's line of sight. For one odd moment, she saw herself in her display and admired her short, spongy hair and her dark skin, which glistened in daylight like a new penny. *Girl, you look good!*

"Stop primping!" Wiki huffed.

Fine. Leen detached a small rubber nub from her headset and gave it to Wiki. "Put that in your ear. That way you can hear me, too."

Wiki did as told and set a course for the Pepperling table.

More people crowded around the supersized veggies, but Wendy had to turn a few away, her cheeks moist. "I'm sorry. I don't have change right now. Could you come back a little later?"

Different folks had different reactions. Clearly, some—a few City Folk, but not all—were miffed, stomping off to other veggie stands. Their need for zucchini apparently couldn't wait. Some asked Wendy if she was okay. She nodded too fast and said, "Allergies."

With a lull in the table traffic, Wiki approached, fighting a laugh as Dewey's legs tickled her collarbone. "Wendy, hey. What happened?"

She faced Wiki, her frizzy mouse-colored hair bouncing as she moved. By the subtle shifts in her face, Wiki knew she was about to say the allergy lie, and didn't want to waste time. "Your cashbox was here, and now it's not. If you want help getting it back, you should tell me what *really* happened."

Wendy's eyes widened, and Wiki—an expert in facial expressions because she could remember and compare *all* of them—saw the girl tick through surprise, suspicion, and fear before settling on hope. "You can help?"

It wasn't *really* a question. The other thing Logan County knew about the Ellison girls was that they helped whenever they could.

Wiki said, "Why are you running your table by yourself? Where'd your dad and brother go?"

"Pa and Walt needed to pick up some things from

Archie's hardware store. Pa was complaining about having to do it after the market, when he'd be tired. I convinced him to go now while I watched over everything."

Wiki understood Wendy's distress. Her family trusted her, and the money had disappeared on her watch. "When do you last remember seeing your cashbox?"

"Right before I had a big rush. I'd just sold some spinach to Mrs. Yeasterly for that spinach-Feta bread she and her husband make, and I sold one onion to Mr. Hannamaker. I gave them both change from my cashbox. When the rush started, so many people were buying things I had a lot of cash in my hand. I was able to make change with what I had, without going to the box. When the rush was over, I went to separate all my bills, but the box was gone." The tears welled again. "Anybody could've taken it."

No. Not anyone. Wiki recalled the rush Wendy had talked about. She only had snapshots of it in her head because she hadn't focused directly on those moments, but she could still identify everyone who'd been around the table. Unfortunately, Wiki had no snapshot of the moment the cashbox disappeared. Her attention had been elsewhere. That didn't mean there weren't clues left behind.

"Wendy, could I take a look behind your table, where the cashbox was?"

"I guess. Normally I'm not supposed to let anyone back here, but what's it matter now?"

Leen spoke through Wiki's earpiece. "If no one was

allowed behind her table, it's highly unlikely someone could've snuck around there without being noticed."

Wiki agreed, examining the area closely. There was a tiny folding table, like the kind Uncle Percy ate off when he had dinner in front of his football games. The cashbox had been there, visible from as far away as the CORN-ucopia. So anyone would've seen it. To actually get to it . . . "A tall person could've reached over, Wendy. Snatched it quick."

The images that Dewey transmitted to Leen's headset allowed her to access augmented-reality measurements that overlaid the scene. In seconds she knew the table's height (29.38 inches), the size of the baskets (three quarts), how many of each vegetable were present (a lot), and so on. Leen made some fast calculations. "Wiki, for a snatch-and-grab like that, the thief would've had to be about six foot two to avoid toppling that pile of tomatoes in front of you and drawing attention."

Wiki sorted through her memory snapshots. Only one among her potential suspects fit.

Leen knew it, too. "Tall like Mr. Hannamaker."

Wiki faced the potato salesman. The mustard stain and moth hole in his shirt were as bold as ever. It made sense that someone struggling with money would be tempted to steal a box full of it. He'd always been such a nice man. "I don't want to believe Mr. Hannamaker is a thief."

Leen said, "Only one way to find out."

✦ ✦ ✦

Wiki approached the potato table cautiously. "Mr. Hanna-maker! Hi!"

He'd been sulking on the stool behind his table, watching shoppers pass by. He perked up at Wiki's presence, his smile nearly splitting his head in half! "Little Miss Ellison. So good to see you. How's your uncle?"

"Sleepy."

"Oh. I certainly understand that. What can I help you with today?"

Wiki giggled and twitched.

Mr. Hannamaker said, "Are you okay?"

More giggling. "I'm fine."

She wasn't. Dewey, making his way down her pant leg, was tickling her again.

Through the earpiece, Leen said, "Distraction time, Wik."

Wiki gathered herself—no more laughs—and asked the question she'd been dreading to say. "How different is a red thumb potato from a French fingerling potato?"

Mr. Hannamaker's smile got even wider. "Vastly different! I'm so glad you asked! See . . ."

While Wiki endured a potato lesson that would wedge into her memory forever, Leen guided Dewey beneath the table, his skittery little legs maneuvering between baskets. It was dusty on the ground, with farmers' market grit clouding Dewey's lenses. Fortunately, Leen's rover upgrades included wipers. She activated them, and they cleared her view, just in time to save Dewey from a collision. Leen skidded him to a stop in front of an object that seemed out of place on the ground, among the gritty potatoes.

Leen said, "I'm looking at a cashbox right now."

Wiki stiffened, while Mr. Hannamaker moved on to the versatility of russet potatoes.

"Hang on," Leen said. "I'm opening it."

Working Dewey's forelegs, Leen undid the box's clasp, lifted the lid. "Oh."

Oh, what? Wiki thought. *Come on, Leen! Tell me something.*

Leen had Dewey check all sides of the box, and double-check the engraving on the underside of the rusted lid. It read: HANNAMAKER FAMILY FARMS, EST. 1964.

"This is *his* cashbox," Leen said. "It's empty."

Wiki only felt small relief. What if Mr. Hannamaker had stashed the Pepperling box elsewhere? Unable to voice her concern without clueing in Mr. Hannamaker, she hoped Leen knew to keep looking.

After Leen made sure the cashbox appeared undisturbed, she arched Dewey up on his hind legs, stretched his forelegs to slowly lower the lid. As she made the delicate move, something else reached over the lid and *grabbed Dewey*. It had eight legs and glowing red lenses, and didn't seem friendly.

It was another rover.

"What the heck!"

Leen's panicked voice frightened Wiki. She turned from Mr. Hannamaker, though he was mid–potato lecture, and stared toward the CORNucopia. Leen waved her off and spoke through the earpiece again. "Keep going. I got this."

Got . . . what? Wiki thought.

Leen refocused on the fight she was in. This rogue red-eyed rover—her own design—was attacking Dewey. *Rude!*

Red Eyes gripped Dewey and tried to overpower him. Leen quickly twisted Dewey into a roll, flinging Red Eyes away. It gathered itself, attacked again, activating tiny pincers on its forelegs, attempting to snip the wires connecting Dewey's AA battery power supply to his servos. If Dewey stopped working, Leen wouldn't be able to help solve the mystery. Time to fight dirty.

Raking one of Dewey's forelegs along the ground, she flung dust directly over Red Eyes's lenses. An old design with no wipers, the rover was blinded. It jerked about, pawed at its lenses with its forelegs, while Dewey circled, then leaped onto its back. Raising his second leg, Dewey activated another new upgrade, and the leg's tip sparked with blue lightning. The rover used his new Taser to shock Red Eyes's power supply, knocking the rover temporarily offline. It fell limp beneath Dewey's weight.

Leen let out a heavy breath that sounded like a hurricane in the earpiece. Wiki glanced toward the CORNucopia while Mr. Hannamaker was telling her, "There are many little-known facts about the Yukon Gold potato . . ."

Leen commanded Dewey to bring his rebellious brother back to the CORNucopia for examination. Then she told Wiki, "Buy a potato and walk away. You need to find Miss Wavers. Now."

Wiki rummaged in her pocket for a dollar bill. "Mr. Hannamaker, I'm sorry to interrupt, but I need to do something for my sister. Could I have a couple of those fingerlings?" She passed the money to him, and he loaded up a small paper bag with more potatoes than she'd paid for.

"Take a few other potatoes so you can see the differences we talked about for yourself."

Wiki felt awful. How could they have thought this sweet man was a thief?

"Thank you," Wiki said gratefully, and moved into the crowd, past Mrs. Honeydew's table, and the busy Yeasterly mini bakery, scanning faces. "Why am I looking for Miss Wavers?"

Leen filled her in on the rover fight, just as Dewey returned with the deactivated rover. "Red Eyes was a rover we sold her."

Still on the move, Wiki concentrated on the ground beneath the Pepperling table. In the dirt were tiny footprints you might mistake for bird prints, maybe field mice. But, really, they were rover prints. That's how the thief had gotten the cashbox.

But *Miss Wavers*?

"It doesn't seem right, Leen. Miss Wavers stealing?"

"I know. It's just, it's her rover."

At the end of the pavilion, perched on a bench in the sunshine, was their new suspect. Miss Wavers saw Wiki coming and greeted her with a sad smile.

"Hi!" Wiki said, understanding Miss Wavers had to be seeing the concern on her face. But nothing prepared Wiki for what the woman said next.

"What's your name, little girl? Are you lost?"

Leen had been in the midst of dismantling Red Eyes when she heard Miss Wavers—who'd known the Ellisons their whole lives—ask for Wiki's name. And Leen felt very afraid. For Miss Wavers.

Wiki felt every bit of the same fear her sister felt. Miss Wavers stared like she'd never seen her before. "Miss

Wavers, I'm Wik—I mean, *Vicki* Ellison. You taught my uncle Percy when he was in third grade."

Wiki might as well have been talking to one of the City Folk who only really saw her when she said their corn was "organic."

There were a number of possibilities for what ailed Miss Wavers. Many conditions affected people's memories to the point where the most familiar things became confused or lost. Alzheimer's, and Parkinson's, and transient ischemic attack, and . . .

No! No, Wiki. You will not glitch. Not now.

She forced herself to focus, in case Miss Wavers needed her help.

"I don't think she did it," Wiki said, unconcerned people would think she was talking to herself. Miss Wavers didn't mind.

"Me neither," Leen said, though for different reasons than Wiki's. "I just took her rover apart. It's full of crumbs. *Bread* crumbs."

In fairy tales, bread crumbs led you home. At the Logan County Farmers' Market, they led you to thieves.

"You know where to meet me," Wiki said. "And bring the market managers."

"I'm putting out the BRB sign now." Leen locked their

cashbox, tucked it into her backpack, then hung a Be Right Back placard on the CORNucopia table.

Wiki said, "Miss Wavers, will you wait right here for me?"

"Sure will, sweetie."

Wading back into the market crowd, Wiki made a bee-line for Mr. and Mrs. Yeasterly's Baked Goods. Their table was crowded as usual, the supply of sticky buns and macarons and savory galettes dwindling. Whenever they ran low, one of the Yeasterlys would disappear into their van, positioned right behind the table, like most vendors'. Only now that she had a reason to be suspicious, Wiki could see what was *really* happening.

Standing in the middle of the market foot traffic, squinting so as not to miss a detail, Wiki focused extra hard on *everything*.

Leen emerged from the crowd, backpack straps cinched tight, with the farmers' market managers behind her. "What you got?"

"All the answers. Let's do this."

Leen and Wiki approached the Yeasterlys with the managers in tow. Mrs. Yeasterly, with her pixie-cut streaked hair, black-framed glasses, and perky demeanor, didn't miss a beat. "Hey there! Jim, it's the Ellison girls and the farmers' market organizers. Come out and say hi!"

The van's door opened, and Mr. Yeasterly leaped out,

shutting it quickly behind him. Not quick enough to stop Wiki from seeing inside and confirming her theory.

Wiki said, "Should I tell, or do you want to do it?"

Leen straightened her AR headset. "I'm handling something right now. It's all you, sis."

"Cool." Wiki spoke loud and clear. "Mr. and Mrs. Yeasterly stole Wendy Pepperling's cashbox, and likely a bunch of other stuff, too."

Mrs. Yeasterly said, "Just wait one darn minute."

"Nope," said Wiki. "Not waiting. Because you're probably instructing your stolen rovers to move the goods right now. Leen, am I wrong?"

"You are not. Got him."

Just then, Dewey leaped from behind a bread box display, carrying a deactivated bot. Wiki said, "The Yeasterlys took Miss Wavers's rover."

Mr. Yeasterly played dumb. "I don't know what that is. I've never seen anything like it before in my life."

The farmers' market managers watched skeptically as Dewey skittered across the table, carrying his hijacked brother. One of the managers said, "Neither have we."

Wiki pointed at the six fat loaves on a rack in the open air. Display loaves. Rye, and wheat, and pumpernickel. All oversized and exposed and crusty so no one would touch them and suspect what they really were. "Those are the same loaves that have been on that rack for two months."

"Of course!" said Mrs. Yeasterly. "They're preserved with polyurethane. It's a common practice. We could use them for two more months."

A manager said, "That is true, Victoria. Most bakers will preserve loaves for display."

Wiki agreed. "Yes. But how many of those bakers hollow their loaves and put hinges on them? Even I didn't notice at first. But I looked closer once I figured out the Yeasterlys had stolen Miss Wavers's rovers and were using them to steal from other vendors."

"That's absurd!" said Mr. Yeasterly. But more like a bad actor in a school play, not like someone who was actually insulted.

Wiki asked the managers, "Have a lot of people been checking the lost and found for stuff lately?"

"Why, yes. Yes, they have."

"Check the bread," said Wiki.

The churning crowd became a lingering one, everyone interested in the disturbance by the baked goods. Among the interested, Wendy Pepperling and Mr. Hannamaker.

Mrs. Yeasterly rounded the table, informed Wiki and the managers, "You will not touch my bread."

Wiki said, "Wasn't talking to them."

Leen directed Dewey to a particularly fat loaf. He ripped the hinges from the back, tossed the crusty top to the ground. The cashbox was hidden inside.

"That," Leen told Wendy, "is yours, I believe."

Wendy rushed forward to claim her stolen money, while Leen maneuvered Dewey to the other display loaves, exposing more stolen goods: jewelry, phones, credit cards and such.

The managers said, "Mr. and Mrs. Yeasterly, we need a word."

But they were gone!

Their van revved to life, the door locks clacked, and they attempted a speedy escape, nearly running over folks.

"They're getting away!" yelled Mr. Hannamaker.

"No, they aren't," Leen said, twitching her eye about quickly behind her AR lens.

The van jerked, made a horrid clanking sound, then coasted to a stop not far from where it'd started. When it was still, several rovers skittered from beneath the vehicle, dragging wires and parts behind them.

Knowing they were beaten, the Yeasterlys left the vehicle with their hands up, and were surrounded by their fellow vendors until the police came.

Leen's rovers returned, skittering up her legs and into her backpack. Many people watched, impressed by this marvelous display, but only one spoke up. He was City Folk, the one with the beard and man bun. He said, "Are those . . . homemade?"

"Guess the secret's out," Wiki said.

Leen rolled her eyes. "Yeah, but they aren't organic, so you probably won't be interested. Now, excuse us. We gotta get back to our table."

"Bye, Miss W!" said Wiki.

Leen said, "Bye, Miss Wavers."

Wiki and Leen had used Miss Wavers's cell phone to call her son, Dave. Now he led her by the hand, guiding her to where his car was parked. Or he tried. She pulled away and came back to the CORNucopia, as if she'd left something.

"Mom," Dave Wavers said, touching her shoulder gently. "We should go."

She remained staring at the twins, unmoving.

"Girls, I'm sorry. She has spells and gets confused," said Dave. "That's the only way those conniving bakers could've nabbed her rovers. I suspect she never even knew they were gone."

Wiki had suspected the same thing, and said, "You don't have to apologize for her."

"Not ever," Leen added.

Some small bit of recognition sparked in the elderly teacher's eyes. "You'll be . . ." She struggled for the words. "You'll be . . ."

"We'll be 'ear' next week," said Wiki, who ignored her sister's wide grin.

Leen said, "We look forward to serving you again."

Miss Wavers and her son got on their way, as did most of the folks under the pavilion. It was after noon, and the market was winding down.

Wendy's brother and dad returned, and she told them what had happened. Pa Pepperling hugged her and said he'd totally trust her to watch the table again.

Mr. Hannamaker had lured Man Bun to his table and convinced him he'd stumbled upon the best organic potatoes in the state, which started a City Folk rush. Mr. Hannamaker sold out of his entire stock. *Good for him.*

Leen and Wiki Ellison sold enough corn to earn their allowances, and get parts for more rovers. Everyone ended up having a good day, except the Yeasterlys, who were going to jail.

Uncle Percy, yawning and stretching like a cat, appeared in time to shut down the CORNucopia. And with his usual question. "What'd I miss?"

The girls, stacking up baskets, being extra careful with the one housing the rovers, didn't miss a beat. "Nothing much."

Rescue

Suma Subramaniam

I hide under my blanket. My stomach is in knots. The last red-orange rays of the sun stream through the window of my bedroom. My heart beats a wild rhythm to the noise downstairs. The loud voices and the screams make my skin crawl. The ears of my yellow lab mix, Duke, twitch as he sits on my bed. His head turns toward the closed door. Appa's anger transforms the brightest of evenings into a dark hollow.

Dhadaar!

That's not a good sound. I imagine Appa throwing the box of murukku from the kitchen countertop onto the floor, the crispy snack fragments scattering.

"Don't you talk to me like that!" Appa yells.

I press my hands into Duke's fur, shaky with fear, and listen to Amma's cries.

The first time I heard Appa yell was four years ago, when I was six. He splashed a hot cup of coffee onto my mother's hands. It was also the first time I saw her weep like a baby. Appa made me promise I would never tell anyone what happened at home.

I was afraid, so I didn't tell anyone what my father did. The burns stayed on Amma's hands for nearly six months.

Appa didn't stop with that. Once, he made my mother touch a hot iron. Another time, my father dropped a box of cereal on her head. I cried out and ran to Amma, but he pushed me away.

"Be quiet!" he yelled.

I couldn't be quiet. I was sobbing loudly. He threatened to drop a big box of oatmeal on me.

Amma resisted. Appa didn't stop.

I wanted to cry even louder, but I shrank. What if he hurt me, too?

"Why is he so mean to you?" I whispered in Amma's ear.

"Your dad is not an evil man, kanna." Her voice went back to normal. "He's struggling, but I cannot excuse his bad behavior."

Her words sat in my heart like a heavy bag of potatoes.

Sometimes Appa is nice to me. He returns from work with a face hanging low, and he is sorry about what he does. Other times, he buys me new dresses, books, candies, and ice cream. I don't know why he switches back and forth so much.

Appa grabs my arms with his big hands. "If you are quiet, Sangeetha, I'll buy anything you want."

Today, I don't want to be quiet. Not when he's beating Amma down again.

I hear something topple from the kitchen counter, then the sound of glass breaking. Appa is shouting, and I hear Amma pleading, "No. Stop it!"

I get off the bed and run to the door. It's locked. Amma locks it sometimes to protect me.

I bang the door. "Amma! Please let me out. Please!"

No one hears me. Duke jumps and scratches the door.

"Down, Duke!" I turn my back on the dog.

He stares at me, confused.

"Good boy," I tell him.

My whole body shakes. I go back to my bed and hide under the blanket again with Duke by my side.

It's summer vacation and I have a lot of time to play, but I can't relax when Appa is shouting. Talking to my dog is the only way I can stay calm.

My parents got Duke before I was born. They adopted him from the local animal shelter because Amma was too lonely when Appa traveled for work and was gone for so many days every month. "Duke is silly and does funny things that make you smile when you are sad. When you talk to him, he will listen," she said to me once. "He'll say stuff back to you in the gentlest ways. There's no such thing as too much love when it comes to a dog."

I hug Duke tight. "When will the yelling stop?" I ask him.

He tilts his head and turns a full circle.

"Duke, when will he stop?" I ask him again.

Duke licks my feet and puts his chin on my lap. He understands me better than Appa does.

I don't sleep at night. I haven't slept for many nights. Appa lost his job last week, and he has been angry since then.

Suddenly I hear footsteps.

"Sangeethaaaaaaaaa!"

Appa's screechy loud voice makes me tremble. If only I could stuff my ears with giant balls of cotton. I jump out of the bed and crawl under it before the door swings open.

Appa barges into the room, shouting, "Sangeetha, come out!"

My heart thumps and I see Amma's feet behind him.

"Come out!" Appa yells. "I know you're hiding."

"Stay there, kanna!" Amma cries.

Appa drags me out and raises his hand. His whiskey breath makes me want to throw up.

Amma tugs at his arm. "Don't do that. She's just a child!"

He lifts his hand to strike my face. I shut my eyes. I can't scream even if it is going to hurt. But Amma stops him.

Duke jumps off the bed and starts barking. His tail winds down toward the floor.

Appa yells over Duke's barks, "You should've come out when I asked you to. Be respectful, Sangeetha."

"But, Appa, you're the one who . . ."

I know he wants me to be quiet, but I can't anymore.

He glares at me. He raises his hand again, but this time, Amma slaps him. "I'm calling the police if you try to touch her again."

Appa shoves her against the wall. "You do that, and they'll take her away. I know what Sangeetha needs better than you do. You don't know how these things work." He turns around and points at me. "You better behave." He slams the door as he leaves the room.

I am shaking, but I don't cry. I don't want Amma to be sadder than she already is. I get on the bed again with Duke. Amma slides her arm, warm, around me. I hold her embrace. I want us to be happy like we are when she reads me a story. I flop on the bed the way Duke does when he's exhausted after a long run.

But Amma doesn't laugh. She keeps a serious face. She adjusts her salwar kameez. "We can't take this anymore. He cannot lash out at you. Wait here, Sangeetha."

I pull at Amma's dupatta. It slides from her shoulder and falls on the bed. "Don't leave me by myself. I'm scared, Amma."

Amma wraps the dupatta across her chest. "I'm going to check on your father and then call your aunt. I'll be back soon."

She locks the door on her way out of the room.

The next morning, I hear a mild creak and the door swings open again. Amma slips into my room before the sun is up.

"We must leave home right now," she whispers in my ear. "Just you and me, Sangeetha. Quick. Let's go."

I rub my eyes and yawn. "What about Duke?"

Duke wakes up, too, and looks at me with his brown eyes, his tongue sticking out.

Amma stares at him with her hand on her chin. "Kadavuley!" Did she forget the dog? "I hate to leave him with your father," she says. "But I don't have a plan now. We can't take Duke with us."

I try to imagine Duke searching for me around the house. It's a depressing image.

Dressed in pajamas, I carry my sneakers and step out. The dog follows me as I tiptoe past my parents' bedroom. I peep through the open door. The room smells of alcohol, like it always does. Appa is sleeping and snoring. He doesn't notice us.

I go to the kitchen. We don't turn on the light. Amma starts packing in the dark and whispers under her breath,

"Get as many things as you can before your father hears anything. We must rush. We don't have time."

We fill a backpack with clothes and snacks. I put bananas into my pockets. I pick up my favorite book, *Charlotte's Web,* which lies on the coffee table. Like Wilbur, I want to fling myself in the mud and weep. But I have to toughen up for Amma. My eyes get watery. I wipe them fast. I slide the book into the backpack. There's no space for anything else.

Duke follows me everywhere. He doesn't leave my side. He was a true friend last night through Appa's screams. He's been there every time Amma locked me in the room. He knows how to keep me warm and safe.

"What will happen to Duke?" I ask Amma again. "If we're not around, who will feed him, walk him, and let him out?"

"No more questions, Sangeetha," says Amma. "Don't cause any more problems than we already have."

"But we can't leave him here. Not with Appa."

"I said no."

"Please, Amma. What if he hurts him, too?"

Amma ignores my words.

I grip her hands. "I can ask Joe. He might say yes." Joe is our neighbor. He is an old man who lives alone. My parents have known him since I was born.

She looks down at her watch and shakes her head. "All

right, kanna . . . seekrama pannu. We need to hurry. You must be quick."

I put Duke on the leash. We step out of the house. Amma closes the door quietly. Outside it's still dark and raining.

I'm worried—we don't know where we're going or what we'll do, but Duke doesn't know that. He pees in the yard, smiles at me, and wags his tail. He thinks we stepped out for a walk. I pet and kiss him, taking in his wet dog smell.

Amma checks on the car. "Take him over to Joe while I load our things, will you?"

Duke and I run over to our neighbor's house. I knock on the door. I've been taking chess lessons from Joe for a year, and in return, Amma makes masala dosas for him. Her rice crepes with coconut chutney and potatoes are his favorite, but I'm not bringing him masala dosas this morning.

Joe agrees to keep Duke for us. "I knew this day would come, Sangeetha. I told your mom I'd help you," he says. "I won't let your dad see Duke. I can hold on to him for a few days. But if I don't hear from you, I'll have to call the animal shelter. I don't have the money to take care of him for too long. I'm sorry."

This is what I know: I trust Joe.

"Will you be okay without Duke?" he asks.

I hand over the leash to Joe. "I'll miss him. And you. Thank you for your help."

"Take care of your mom, sweetie."

I shake Joe's hand. "I'll remember the chess analysis tips you taught me."

He gives me a firm handshake with his warm hands. "Good, kiddo! Remember—take notes of your moves. Recognize your patterns."

"Sure!" My eyes turn to Duke. "He likes peanut cookies. If you give him one every day, he'd be so grateful."

Joe smiles. "I know Duke's favorites. You find a place to settle down. We'll be seeing you then."

Duke pulls on his leash and whines. I swallow my tears and leave without looking back. I go to our driveway, where Amma's car is parked. Drizzle falls on my face. The raindrops mist my cheeks like the dew that pearls over Amma's rosebushes.

Amma races over to me and tugs my arm. "Hurry up, Sangeetha! We have to leave before your dad wakes up."

I get into the car. Amma pulls out of the driveway. We pass Joe's house. The door is closed. At the corner of the street, I roll down the window and glance back at our house one last time. I don't see Appa. What will he do if he finds out that Duke is with Joe?

I sit with my arms crossed over my chest. It's warm in the car. I already miss Duke. My world is so gloomy. All I want is a happy family. I don't want to feel scared and anxious about my parents all the time. I wish things were different. But what am I to do?

Amma doesn't talk. On any other day, she'd launch

into a fun conversation, but today, it's deadly silence. We drive away from our neighborhood, and then we're out on a back road. After a while, I notice that Amma is driving in circles.

"Where are we going?" I ask her many times.

She puts her hand to her face. She's on the verge of crying. "Don't ask me anything, Sangeetha."

"Amma," I whisper, and lean toward her seat.

She tightens her grip on the steering wheel and stares at the road. She wipes the tears that roll down her face and continues driving.

"Please, Amma. Don't cry."

She doesn't speak. I have to do something. So I start to sing. I sing to her all the songs I know so she feels better. I'm not sure it's helping, but I sing anyway.

Somehow time flies by quickly. Amma pulls the car over in a park. She turns off the ignition.

"Where are we going?" I ask her again.

"I talked to Mina chithi last night. She has invited us to stay with her."

"Mina chithi?"

She nods. "Just until we figure out something for ourselves."

I've never met Mina chithi. All I know is that Aunt Mina is my mother's distant cousin. But I've heard Amma talk to her on the phone.

Amma turns to me. "We're going south," she says. "Houston, Texas. Our new home. Where Mina lives."

I try to imagine Houston. I know that the weather is warmer there, and it's home to the NASA Space Center. I try to imagine Mina chithi's house. But all I see is Duke and the street outside my home in Seattle. I put my hand to my forehead and try to stay calm.

Amma's phone dings. Joe's sending a text and a picture of Duke.

Don't worry about Duke. I really hope you're safe and all is well.

I look at my dog's picture on the phone. He's smiling. My brain is spinning. I'm angry that I had to leave Duke even though none of this is my fault.

Amma starts the car. We keep driving from one town to the other. From apple orchards to parks to vineyards to the woods to dry lands. We drive for hours. Hours spread into a day. I miss Duke. My throat chokes. I can tell Amma is tired from the driving. Every time we stop for gas, she's counting the dollars. She's scared to use her credit card.

"What if your dad finds out where we are? We can't be a family again, Sangeetha."

"Love you, Amma. I'm sorry." I pause. "But I worry that we shouldn't have left Duke behind."

Amma changes the conversation. "Well, Mina chithi's house is only a thirty-five-hour drive from Seattle," she says. "Plenty of new adventures ahead of us."

"But Duke isn't with us. How are we going to be happy without him?"

Amma has no answer.

My throat tightens. I can no longer pretend to be calm. I dig into my backpack and eat the last of the bananas. The fruit is overripe. I mash it between my teeth and let the sweetness heal the cracks in my heart.

We stay on the road until Amma says that we have little money left. It's evening, and I'm hungry. I look into my backpack again. We've run out of the granola bars, the homemade murukku, and ribbon pakoda snacks. I put the empty plastic bags and snack wrappers in a bag to throw away later. "I wonder if Joe's giving Duke a cookie right now."

"Kadavuley!" she says, as if the gods can help. "There are six missed calls from your appa."

"Are you going to call him back?"

Amma shakes her head. "I hope your father doesn't see Duke. I also feel bad for leaving the pooch behind."

"Duke will be all right," I tell her. "Joe promised to take good care of him."

"Sangeetha, listen." Amma's voice grows low. "Whatever happens with me and your father, I will do everything I can to keep you safe. I promise we'll get through this together."

My eyes begin to sting. "Appa scares me. But I miss Duke even more."

"Sorry, kanna," Amma mutters. "I know you do. But I'm here for you now. Okay?"

I don't say anything. I simply nod. Amma's words don't help.

We drive through snowcapped mountains. The air gives me chills and cracks my lips. The rough wind pierces my skin, making it dry.

Joe sends another text.

Duke is well. Thinking about you two. Take care.

My head hurts. Amma is tired from the driving.

"Are you and Appa going to divorce?" I ask.

Amma takes her time to reply. "I don't know yet, kanna. Let's just say our marriage is not working."

"You mean you can't stand each other?"

Amma chokes. "It's complicated. But we have to move on."

Sadness brews inside me. I rub my eyes and look out the window, trying hard not to cry.

At night, Amma parks the car in an empty parking lot off the freeway near Boise. She pulls out a good warm blanket from the trunk. The night sky is filled with stars. We fold down the back seats and make our bed a cocoon of comfort. We try to sleep. I miss snuggling up with Duke. Would he be sleeping at Joe's feet?

In the morning, we're back to driving again. We stop at a rest area on the freeway. My stomach rumbles. Amma buys me a burger. I wasn't expecting a home-cooked breakfast. Piping hot, fluffy steamed idli or deep-fried vadai. Spicy sambar and coconut chutney. Nope. But I'd rather eat a sugary bowl of cereal. A burger? It's cheap, I know. Amma buys an extra one for the road.

When we're just about to leave, we see a woman outside the store, waving to us. Her hair is scruffy, and her clothes are dirty. She has a puppy, too . . . a black one with some white on the upper body and parts of his legs and feet. I can't tell the breed, but the dog is sturdy, and big-boned like Duke.

"I'm Grace," the woman says, and she points to her puppy. "He's Buddy."

Buddy moves his empty food bowl around with his nose and barks. He sniffs my hand. He is hungrier than I am. I give the extra burger to the woman. She divides it in half and shares it with the dog.

I pet Buddy. He licks my fingers with his soft tongue. He wears a cross around his neck. It reminds me of Duke's tag, with its picture of Ganesha, the Hindu elephant-headed god, remover of obstacles. Every evening, Amma would light an oil lamp before the pictures of deities at the household altar. We'd chant the Gayatri Mantra while Duke curled by my feet. I would press my palms together in prayer and close my eyes. I like the sounds of the mantra. Our chanting would waft through the room and comfort us on difficult days.

I want to help Grace and her dog, but we don't have any money. I whisper into Amma's ear. "Could we take them along with us? Doesn't look like they have a car."

Amma catches my eye and nods. She turns to Grace. "We can drop you on our way. Do you have anywhere to go?"

"Where are you headed?" Grace asks.

"Texas," Amma replies.

Grace shakes her head. "Could you drop me at Provo? I have a friend in Utah." She straightens her tattered shirt and loose jeans.

"Come on, then," says Amma.

The warmth of helping floods me. I love it when Amma is this way.

We get into the car. Grace sits in the front, while Buddy sits with me in the backseat.

All of us are quiet except Buddy. When Amma rolls the window down, he sticks his face out and sniffs the air. I sneeze and wish I could enjoy the wind like he does.

"What breed is he?" I ask Grace.

"He's an Alusky," she says. "A mix of Alaskan malamute and Siberian husky."

I pet his soft fur. "Ooh! That's fancy. No wonder he looks like a wolf dog."

Grace laughs. "I get that a lot. I was lucky to find him abandoned on the road five years ago. He's a good dog."

She has a catchy laugh.

"Buddy reminds me of Duke," I tell her.

"Who's Duke?" Grace asks.

"My dog," I say. "He's in Seattle right now. With my neighbor."

"Why is he with your neighbor?"

I look up at Amma and then at Grace. "My dad's out of town. So our neighbor takes care of Duke whenever we're away," I say, although it is not the truth. This is the first time we've left Duke with Joe. I see Amma raising her eyebrows at me in the rearview mirror. I shrug. Lying is not okay, but I know we cannot share our story with a stranger.

"Oh!" Grace smiles. "What breed is Duke?"

"A lab-shepherd mix," Amma replies. "I got him from a local rescue. Adopting Duke was one of the best decisions I made."

"You bet," Grace agrees. "I can't imagine life without Buddy. He makes every day a bit better."

I ask for Amma's phone. There are no messages from Joe. Perhaps Duke misses me, too.

At a rest area in the afternoon, I open my bag and search for something, anything to eat. But there's absolutely nothing.

Grace gives me a packet of potato chips. "Here you go," she says. "I have two of these."

Grace seems nicer than Appa, and she smiles a lot. I can't imagine Appa smiling when things aren't going right.

I look down at the phone, and now there's a text from Joe.

Walked Duke. Hope everything's okay!

I write back:

On our way to Houston. We're well.

Buddy rolls over on his back for a belly rub and makes me laugh. He's as goofy as Duke.

Grace gets out of the car near a traffic signal in Provo.

"Will you be staying here?" I ask.

"If my friend's okay with it, yeah. But I can't let Buddy go. I'll have to find a way to keep him. He's all I got," Grace replies.

Amma and I exchange a look, but she quickly turns her

face and stares at the small Ganesha idol that's stuck on the dashboard. I wish we also could find a way to keep Duke.

Grace gives me her other packet of potato chips. "A small gift for you to remember me."

I hold the packet in one hand and ruffle Buddy's fur with the other. He jumps up and gives me a slurpy kiss. His drool is all over me, and I giggle.

Grace thanks Amma and squeezes my shoulder. "Give your pup a cuddle for me, okay, kiddo?"

I nod, remembering Duke's sweet smile.

After Grace leaves, Amma checks the phone. Joe has sent a video of Duke chasing a rabbit in his yard. We laugh at his goofiness. Then she starts driving again.

I need a plan. I have to convince Amma to go back to Seattle for Duke.

"You know what I'd do when we see Duke again?"

"Yeah?" Amma asks.

"I'd give him a squishy hug. He'd pounce on me, lick my chin, and his tail would go round and round. 'Hi, Dukey! I got you a cookie.' That's what I'd say to him."

Amma laughs. "Because there are three simple ways to gain his love—give food, show food, have food."

"How much farther?" I ask.

She says, "I'll look at the map. But you know what? I need a break from the driving. Let's take a walk. I saw an exit sign for a lake. It's nearby."

I grin. Amma and I often used to take the lake trail by our house. Duke would play with his dog pals there.

But today, when we reach the lake, the water is not calm. The wind is strong. The waves remind me of Appa's anger. And the whole time, I feel sorry about Duke.

We sit on a bench under the cloudy sky, watching dog walkers pass by. I clear my throat. It's cold and my teeth are chattering, but I seize the moment anyway.

I hold Amma's hand. I have to say it without making her cry. "I know we just got away from Appa, and you may not want to return. But Duke . . . he's my best friend, Amma. We both need him." I get down on my knees. "Please, Amma. Could we go back for him?"

Amma taps my shoulder and shakes her head. "Oh, Sangeetha."

I look up at her eyes. I don't say anything.

I wait.

She sighs and pauses for a moment.

I still don't say anything. I want to understand how she feels more than what she thinks.

Amma goes down on her knees, too, and hugs me tight. "Okay," she says. "You are right, kanna. We cannot go away like this. Seeing Grace, it just reminded me of you and Duke. He's family. He needs you as much as I do."

Tears stream down my cheeks. "Are we going back to Seattle, then?"

Amma wipes my face. She takes my chin in her palm and smiles. "We'll need to make sure your father doesn't spot us. Let's go get Duke. There's no such thing as too much love when it comes to him. No matter what, Duke will go with us wherever we go from here."

The sun shines through the clouds and glimmers over the waves hitting the shoreline. Amma takes out her phone and snaps a picture of the pink lemonade sky. "The scenery is gorgeous, isn't it?"

Amma's words are a balm to my ears. "Couldn't be better. I am so happy we are going back to Seattle, Amma." My voices cracks as I hold her hand. "I am so happy we're going back for Duke."

The Save

Joseph Bruchac

Oren shifted the stick from one hand to the other. Usually that was no big deal. Right now it felt heavy as a sledge-hammer. Even with the mask on his face, his padding, and his gloves, he was feeling naked. The goal behind him was the standard six feet by six feet, but it seemed as big as a barn door now that he was the one guarding it.

In front of him in their various positions ranged nine other Onondaga boys on their team. Paul Hemlock, who had the wingspan of an eagle and who was even taller than their coach, was to his right. Paul's face, as usual, looked serious, even though he was always the first to crack a joke after the game was over. To Oren's far left was Billy Crouse, who was always grinning. He was much faster than he looked and their best defender. Perry Elm, the third defender and closest, turned to look over his shoulder at Oren.

"No worries," Perry said. "We got this. No one's getting past us."

Oren nodded. He was actually on the same field with these guys, in a real game. His heart should have been pumping with excitement. He'd finally been given the opportunity to play the position he'd practiced for so very long. Instead, what he felt inside his chest seemed like a lump of lead.

Why am I so upset?

Nothing was at stake now. They were ahead 14–2. Only two minutes left. *No way we can lose. No way.* He mouthed those words for the fourth or maybe the fifth time. *No way we can lose. No way.* That was why he, the third-string goalkeeper, had been given a chance.

A chance to look like a bum.

The team they were playing, the Buffalo Bulls, actually wasn't that bad. His own guys were so far ahead because they had gone on a mad scoring streak. Although, to be honest, his team also was winning because they were a whole lot better. After all, the Bulls weren't buffalos at all. They were just city kids.

He'd bet none of them had ever set foot on a lacrosse field before they hit middle school. How many of them had held their first stick before they could even walk? How many of them had a grandfather like his who was a legend and an All-American? And not one of those kids on the visiting team was Indian.

While we invented the game. We are the Iroquois.

We are the Iroquois,
we're proud, we are strong

That's how Joanne Shenandoah sang it on his mom's favorite CD. How it sounded on the playlist on Oren's own iPhone. It was sort of a corny song, but it usually inspired him way more than Jay-Z's latest rap.

Iroquois. We're Iroquois. And everybody on our team is head and shoulders above these guys.

Except me.

For some reason, even though he was trying to concentrate, his mind wandered back to when they were showing those Buffalo kids around. Maybe because he was a third-stringer, he'd been one of the members of his team delegated to be a tour guide. A way to make him feel more useful, he guessed.

He almost laughed remembering the reactions of those city boys when they were given the short tour of the Rez before the game. The best moment came when they were taken up onto the hill to see the tribal buffalo herd grazing on the yellow autumn grass in the wide field.

"Wow," one of the kids said, a stocky boy who turned out to be their overmatched goal tender. "Those are real!"

"Realer buffalos than we are," said the kid who'd been standing next to Oren. He was tall and lanky. Rajat was his name, the only name Oren seemed to remember from among them. There was a sort of British accent in the precise English he spoke. Oren had liked him for his politeness. Then he liked him even more for the sense of humor he showed again when he leaned over toward Oren and said, "I, too, am Indian. But of another sort entirely—transposed, you might say." He flipped one hand over the other. "American Indian. Indian American."

A third kid, whose hair was cut so short it looked like a newly mowed lawn, reached out to pluck one of the heavy braided-steel cables strung between the iron girders that served as posts for the fence around the field. "Do they ever get out of there?" he said. He sounded nervous.

"Yup," said Bill Jimmerson, the keeper of the herd, who was leading this part of the tour. "But only when they want to."

That was when the buffalo everyone on the Rez called Big Guy, the largest male in the herd, decided to show *his* sense of humor. He spun around and charged—hooves pounding like a powwow drum—straight at the gathered crowd, nostrils flaring, head down. His snorting was loud as a trumpet as he thudded toward them.

To their credit, not all of the Buffalo Bulls and their various coaches and chaperones ran or tripped over their own feet as they tried to flee.

As usual, Big Guy stopped inches away from the fence, his hooves throwing up clods of dirt and brown grass as he skidded to a halt. Then he lowered his head so that Bill Jimmerson could reach through the fence to scratch behind his horns.

"I believe," said Rajat, who'd remained next to Oren, "that this one does not wish to get out yet."

The visiting lacrosse kids recovered quickly.

"Wow," said a thin, long-armed kid whose sweatshirt had a design of crossed sticks and the number 10. He was shaking his head and smiling as he stepped back up to the fence. "That is how to charge the goal."

"You bet, Masterson," said the slightly shorter boy by his side. Like his friend, he'd stepped back a few paces but hadn't fled for his life when Big Guy mock-charged. The shorter boy's sweatshirt bore a large number 7.

Number 7.

A whistle sounded.

Wake up!

Oren looked up the field. The ball had been put back into play.

There actually were a couple of pretty darn good players on that Buffalo team. Numbers 10 and 7. The two kids who'd admired Big Guy. The fastest of the three attackers. They'd scored the only goals. One each against Lee Elm, his team's second-string goalie. Those two scores were impressive. Lee was almost as good as Phil Mohawk and would for sure be guarding the net next year after Phil graduated.

Number 10 and Number 7. Both of them were now heading Oren's way at a fast lope, passing the ball back and forth between them. He bet they were setting up some variation of the plays they'd scored on before.

Be a panther in the goal.

That was how his grandfather and namesake put it to him.

Oren crouched. He could feel his heart beating now. It was pounding so hard it was as if an eagle were trying to fight its way out of his chest.

Numbers 10 and 7 were crisscrossing in front of him, trying to draw him one way or the other. Oren stayed in his crouch.

A panther. Be a panther, he thought.

Number 10 had the ball.

Masterson, Oren remembered. *That's his name.*

Everything was in slow motion now. Masterson was reversing his stick to make a shot over his back shoulder. Oren had seen him work that move with success twice before. The ball was about to leave the webbing just as Number 7 charged Oren.

Oren tried to leap, lacrosse stick extended to stop the shot. But as he did so, his feet crossed and his legs tangled together, at the exact moment when Number 7 ran into him.

Oren flipped in midair and landed flat on his belly. He couldn't move. The wind had been knocked out of him like a piece of Bubble Wrap tromped on by a boot.

I really am a bum was all he could think.

He gasped, struggling to regain his breath.

A whistle sounded.

The game was over. People were shouting.

"All right!"

"What a move!"

"Great!"

They're praising that goal scored while I was belly flopping, Oren thought.

Then he realized the voices were those of his own teammates.

And it was not just his own guys who'd been impressed. Number 10 and Number 7 were leaning down on either side of him.

"Man," Number 10—Masterson—said as the two Buffalo players lifted him to his feet. "That was amazing!"

Oren looked down at the stick he was still clutching with his left hand. There, held in the webbing like an eagle's egg in its nest, was the ball.

Coach White was patting him on his shoulder.

"Oren, my man, you may be Phil's slot next season," the coach said.

I should tell everyone it was an accident, Oren thought. But he didn't.

My door is always open. That was what his grandfather always said to Oren.

And it was. When Oren got to his grandfather's cabin, the door wasn't locked. But his grandfather wasn't there.

There was a note on the door.

> Gone to council meeting
> Come on in
> Foods in the fridge

Oren pushed the door open and went straight to the fridge.

He was sitting at the kitchen table, finishing off his fourth piece of fried chicken, when his grandfather arrived.

"Sge:no," his grandfather said. It was the old greeting, a word that simply meant "peace."

"Sge:no," Oren replied.

"Leave me any of that bird?" his grandfather said, chuckling as he pulled up a chair and reached for the plate.

"Not much," Oren admitted.

"No problem," his grandfather replied as he picked the meat off the one wing Oren had missed. "Plenty more at Firekeepers. Still hungry?"

Oren nodded. These days he was always hungry. Probably because of that growth spurt his mom said he was about to have. Which would likely end up with him being taller than his uncle Lee. That growth spurt couldn't come fast enough as far as Oren was concerned. He was tired of being half a head shorter than the other boys on the team.

"Ready?" his grandfather said, standing up and gesturing with his chin at the door.

"Born ready," Oren replied.

The two of them set off walking.

It wasn't that far to Firekeepers. No more than a mile. It was the restaurant where everyone on the Rez liked to eat, even if the four-lane road that had been cut a generation ago through their community was only two hundred yards from the parking lot. After all, it was Indian-owned and served fry bread almost as good as his mom made.

They sat at their usual table. So usual that the waitress— one of the teenage Thompson twins who looked so alike Oren could never tell them apart—brought out the plate of fry bread, two bowls of buffalo chili, and two glasses of water without their having to order.

"Anything else?" Mary or Margie said, wiping her hands on her apron.

"Nope," his grandfather said. "Nya:weh."

"Nya:weh," Oren said, echoing his grandfather's thanks.

The fry bread and chili vanished about as fast as a gray squirrel scooting around a tree trunk. They sat there for a while in companionable silence.

"Wish I could have been at the game today rather than that council meeting," his grandfather finally said, looking out the open window to their right, where one of the Jemison boys was trying to start his stubborn three-wheeler. "Heard you made a great play."

Oren shook his head. He'd hoped his grandfather hadn't heard about it. But he should have known. News of anything you did—whether good or bad—traveled around the Rez at warp speed.

"No," Oren said.

His grandfather didn't say anything. He just looked at Oren, raising an eyebrow.

Oren took a deep breath. Then he explained it all, how it had been nothing more than a happy accident. How he felt like a fraud. How he didn't deserve any praise at all.

His grandfather just listened. Then he waved at the waitress behind the counter.

"Hey, Margie," he said. "Got any of that herbal tea?"

"Coming up, Big O," she replied.

His grandfather smiled at Oren. "Know how to tell them apart?"

Oren shook his head.

"Mary is the one with the beauty mark on her right cheek. Margie's is on the left and half an inch higher."

His grandfather sipped his tea. Outside in the parking lot the Jemison boy was banging the motor of his ATV with a wrench.

Oren waited. There was no point in trying to rush his grandfather. He watched as the old man finished his tea, sighed, and then lifted his right hand to rub his chin.

"What was it you intended to do other than stop that shot?" he said. "And what did you end up doing?"

"Gramps, all it was," Oren said, "was dumb luck."

His grandfather shook his head. "I think it was more than that. I've watched you practice. You have good reflexes. Sometimes we can do things that surprise even ourselves. Plus, what's wrong with luck? If I had to choose, my goal would be to have somebody on my team who's lucky any day of the week."

Oren stood up. He wasn't sure why, maybe just that it was hard for him to sit and listen to his grandfather's words trying to convince him he wasn't the loser he knew himself to be.

What happened next was hard for even Oren to explain. Just that there was a loud bang and a spurt of fire from the Jemison boy's ATV, followed by something whizzing through the air toward them. And that somehow Oren found himself flying—like a big cat—right over the table, knocking his grandfather to the floor as a shard of sharp metal spun over their heads.

"Gramps," Oren said, jumping to his feet and looking down at his grandfather lying on his back. "Are you okay?"

His grandfather smiled up at him. "Better than I would have been if that hit me," he said, looking toward where the piece of metal was buried in the restaurant wall.

Suddenly there were people all around them.

"You see what that boy did?"

"I never saw the like."

His grandfather held out a hand and let Oren help him up.

"Well," he chuckled, "nya:weh, Grandson. Thank you! Remember what I said about you having good reflexes? No way are you going to feel bad about this save."

"I guess so." Oren grinned.

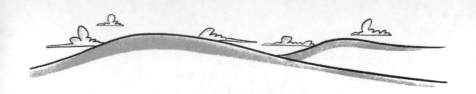

Los Abuelos, Two Bright Minds

Juana Medina

There's nothing I love more than having onces with my abuelos. While they drink coffee and eat achiras, I drink chocolate milk and eat calados with butter and honey.

We sit in my abuela's studio, facing the large windows that make it the warmest room in their house.

Resting our plates on her drawing table, we see way beyond their garden, as the Andes Mountains become gigantic shadows and the sun disappears.

I often worry about my abuelos. My abuelo says they are not *that* old. But I know they aren't young. Also, Abuela's heart isn't strong. She got sick when she was little. She was so horribly ill that days of high fevers affected her heart.

Abuela might not be strong enough to climb mountains, but she's courageous. She's been through so many heart surgeries, the kind where they open your chest as if they're unzippering it, breaking ribs to get to the heart. Despite all the pain she's had, Abuela is always laughing about something, her deep laughs filling the room with a hearty roar.

One time I asked Abuela when she had been the happiest in her whole life. She said, "I remember running like the wind when I was six years old. After that, I was too sick to even stand or walk. I was stuck in bed endlessly. But thankfully, there's too much to do and appreciate, even if you have to stay lying down! Stacks of books started quickly accumulating by my bedside, as I decided to read and learn all I could about the world."

Abuela loves history and architecture. She couldn't go to college because of her weak heart, but being endlessly curious and hungry for knowledge, she found ways to learn about mechanics and beautiful designs. In her woodshop, she built puzzles and clocks and even sailboats. Abuela is an extraordinary engineer.

She might not have a strong beating heart, but she's determined. Like the hummingbirds that visit her garden, Abuela's body might be delicate and often need rest, but she's an amazing builder.

Abuela says, "Throughout my life, I've had to stay still, but your abuelo has always been on the move. When he was little, he dreamed of being a pilot. With help from his siblings, he'd jump off the roof of his house, inside an enormous cauldron, landing safely on the leafy abutilons and fig trees planted in the garden."

That surely got him into serious trouble! His mom—my great-grandma—didn't like the idea of him jumping off roofs . . . and even less, the idea of him becoming a pilot.

Eventually, my abuelo gave up on the idea of flying, and instead became a medical doctor, a brain surgeon.

Over our onces in the late afternoon, as we watch birds eating from the feeders my abuelos have built, Abuelo tells me about how he left Colombia to study in Chicago. Abuela wipes from her fingers the fine crumbs left behind by the achiras. She gets up and leaves the woodshop while Abuelo is describing Chicago—a magical place where he found his love for blues and jazz, and where he enjoyed meeting people with unique and extraordinary stories. He loved living there, but he also found it very hard. Especially in the cold weather. Sometimes, even spring-like Bogotá feels cold to him. That's why he likes his cafecito boiling hot and he wears a puffy jacket inside the house.

Abuela comes back holding a large tin box full of old pictures. She takes out a photo of a tall man with dark hair. He's wearing a white coat, and his legs are halfway buried in snow. That surely isn't Bogotá!

I read the inscription on the back: *Fernando, 1953.*

Abuelo tells me about how he used to shovel coal after his long surgery shifts. He worked back-to-back shifts so he could sleep on empty gurneys instead of having to pay housing rent.

I ask Abuelo why he had to work all the time.

They both sit quietly for a while. Abuelo explains. "While I was studying neurology in Colombia, I went back home to find out everything had been burnt to ashes. After a prominent presidential candidate was murdered, there were violent riots in Bogotá. The city was on fire, Juani." He pauses.

"We lost everything."

"My grandfather's chemistry books had been destroyed. My sisters' toys had melted. My parents were left hopeless. I was the oldest son. I promised myself I would do everything I could to help my family rebuild their home and get back on their feet. I was young and I didn't know how to help my family. I went to a place where I'd often found answers to my questions: the library." There, a librarian friend told Abuelo of scholarships available to study abroad. Diligently, he applied to as many as he could.

Abuelo received a prestigious scholarship that allowed him to follow his dream: to keep learning about the human brain while helping his family. He packed his few belongings, and after a difficult goodbye, he left home.

"A small plane, so flimsy it appeared to be scratching its belly on the Andes Mountains, flew me from Bogotá to coastal Barranquilla. Once I recovered my strength from that flight, I jumped on a steamboat, which battled its way up the furious Magdalena River, where caimans rested on its shores." Docking in Panama, he boarded a new plane with a further destination: Miami. "Once in Miami, I flew to Chicago, my home for the next couple of years." This adventure lasted weeks. Today, I'd need less than ten hours to leave Bogotá and comfortably land in Chicago!

The journey was nothing short of miraculous!

Abuela has heard this story a million times, but she's not bored by it. While she sips her coffee, she sketches a new project she's working on. Every now and then she lifts her head and tells me something else about the old pictures, or laughs heartily at Abuelo's remarks.

They know each other so well. Better than I'll probably get to know anyone in my life!

Abuelo was often told by friends and family that he shouldn't marry Abuela. After all, she was quite sick, and many doctors said she wouldn't live long. But Abuelo loved her fierce drive and enormous curiosity. When Abuelo proposed to Abuela, he gave her a delicate watch with a sophisticated automatic mechanism. This watch only needed the slight movement of the wearer's wrist to keep working.

"I told your abuela I'd love to spend every minute of my life with her."

Then I noticed Abuela's wrist. How she moved her wrist while she ate her achiras and brushed away the crumbs. How she moved her arms gracefully as she looked through pictures, sharing their history with me. How every drawing she made gave her watch more time to beat.

Your abuelo likes to say that it's my beat that keeps us going strong. I think it is just doing what we love to do.

My abuelos have helped a lot of people. After living for many years in Chicago, New Orleans, and Boston, they returned to Colombia. Abuelo was one of the first brain surgeons in the country. Many patients urgently needed operations, but there was no equipment for Abuelo to perform surgery.

Abuela was quick to find a solution: she helped design and build surgical equipment with dedication and utmost precision.

Building surgery equipment was their first collaboration. Now they build birdhouses together for the blackbirds, hummingbirds, and orioles that visit their garden.

It's not just birds (and me!) who visit my abuelos. Many friends and important guests visit. That's how I've met Nobel laureates, important scientists, and highly revered doctors. Everyone has a fascinating story. But Abuelo's favorites are his former patients. They come from all walks of life: farmers, photographers, dancers, teachers . . . even a president.

Abuelo was known for performing operations without charging his patients. He says, "I can't just sit still when there's a way to help a sick person." His patients often bring him heartfelt presents. Cheese from their farms, fresh flowers, original paintings, or knitted scarves.

People love my abuelos because of their giving nature and generous spirit.

On my visits, I enjoy their great stories. Abuelo taught me how to tie my shoes and write my name. He's always telling me, "Juani, find out how things work. Stay curious!" Abuela tells me to see beauty everywhere, even in the smallest things. I promise that no matter what happens, I'll remember this always. Just like the watch Abuelo gave Abuela, every little nudge they give me keeps me going.

Thrown

Mike Jung

Attacking Anika Sensei during aikido instruction is awesome because she does throws better than anyone. I mean, obviously—she's the *teacher*. That's why we call her "sensei."

I wasn't the only one hoping to attack—Martha Bee was bouncing in place so hard that I could feel the floor vibrating. I can't always tell what people next to me are doing, but when Martha's in Energizer Bunny mode it's hard to not tell.

"Martha, please sit in a good seiza," Anika Sensei said.

Seiza is how we sit in aikido—legs under us, toes pointing back, knees apart, hands on thighs, and no bouncing. Martha stopped. Mostly.

"Ryo kata tori kokyu nage tenkan! Stevie, please!"

Yeah! I slapped my hands and forehead down in a bow, jumped up, and ran across the cushioned blue mats until I was facing Sensei from ten feet away. The other aikido kids sat in line to my left, watching, which used to make me nervous when I was new.

Sensei dropped her arms to her sides and I ran at her, reaching for her shoulders. Just as I got there, she stepped sideways and toward me, pushed my right arm down, tucked her hand under my left elbow, and threw me. I tucked my head into my chest and rolled across the mats and onto my feet, facing back at Sensei. I attacked again and she threw me again from the other side. I sprang up again and she held up a palm, so I flopped into seiza.

"This technique starts with a double shoulder grab," Anika Sensei said. I kept my eyes on her as she explained the move—there were two new students, Anna somebody and Linnea somebody, so Sensei talked more than usual. Then we demonstrated again.

"Thank you, Stevie." Sensei turned back to the class. "With a partner."

Everyone bowed, and I hurried over to Martha, who was bouncing again. I'm older than her—I'm eleven, she's ten—but only by four months, and we're both red belts, so we're evenly matched. I backed onto the mats and waited. Martha set her feet, pushed up her glasses with a thumb, and charged. *Bam,* turn, *kapow,* knock down her arm, and *whoosh,* do a perfect throw.

Aikido. It's the best thing ever.

I know I've been at Twin Rivers Aikido for two years because every year Anika Sensei sends certificates saying how long we've been there. You don't get a red belt unless you're good, so when Anika Sensei said I could start going to teen and adult class, I was excited but not surprised. I didn't say so, though. We're supposed to be all humble and stuff.

"You're ready," Anika Sensei said. We were sitting in seiza, facing each other.

"Thank you, Sensei."

"Questions?"

I like how Anika Sensei doesn't rush me while I figure out what to say. Even Mom and Dad do it sometimes, but the worst Anika Sensei does is tell me to think about it and ask again later.

"Will we practice weapons every time like we do here?"

"Teens and adults have a separate weapons class; you can definitely attend, but you'll get lots of practice here."

"Hai." That's Japanese for "yes." It's also kind of like saying "Aye, aye, Captain" to your sensei.

"Anything else?"

"Do you go to the teen and adult classes?"

"Not all of them, but I'll be there on Tuesday evenings."

Good to know. We turned at the sound of more kids arriving. Martha was already inside with her equipment bag and weapons case, Trinity was bowing in, and Sofia and Malik were giggling about something just outside the door.

"I'll let you get back to warming up." Anika Sensei bowed—her bows were very precise—and stood up.

"Hai, Sensei." I bowed, too, then ta-da! Martha was there.

"Hey! So?"

"So . . . what?"

"You're so funny. When do you start teen and adult classes?"

"Tuesday."

Martha began stretching her legs. "Awesome! Is Arthur here?"

Martha Bee and Arthur Levit were the two people I had already known before starting aikido. In third grade Arthur and I were in the same class for the first time, and when Martha moved to town, she was put in there, too.

"Nope."

"Humph." Martha pressed the sole of her right foot against the inside of her left leg and grabbed her toes.

"He's probably tired from the trip."

"Probably. It's weird that you'll be training with my mom."

"I like your mom."

Martha's mom is one of the only adults besides my sensei and my parents who talk about autism without making me feel bad.

"Me too—I mean, duh, she's my mom—but you've been doing aikido longer, so you're probably way better!"

" 'Probably'? Don't you know?"

"We're in different classes, you know." Martha sat up, brought the soles of her feet together, and leaned forward.

"It's weird that I'll train with your mom before you do."

"Yup!" Martha leaned forward on her hands and frog-hopped up onto her feet. "Let's practice rolls!"

We spread out, and as I dropped my arm, tucked my head, and rolled, I felt superconfident. Plus, I'd finally get to learn from Brandon Sensei, who was autistic too. Autistic me learning from an autistic teacher was the whole reason Mom had suggested Twin Rivers Aikido in the first place. How hard could teen and adult class be?

News flash: teen and adult class was SO HARD.

I knew the tall black belt facing me was named Kristof—I'd seen him at the dojo community dinners—but I hadn't trained with him before. We first did a technique where you pivot, raise your arms, and do a throw that's basically a mutant elbow strike. I'd done it literally hundreds of times. Easy-peasy, right?

WRONG. Kristof's arm fell from the sky like a sawed-off tree. Instead of doing a side fall, whirling my legs, and getting up, I buckled like an accordion, got my feet crossed, and toppled onto my back. I staggered as I got back up.

Why was Kristof smiling? I've practiced telling what it means when people do specific things with their faces and I'm good at it, but I couldn't tell why he was smiling. Maybe I was too distracted by his superbristly beard.

When it was my turn to throw Kristof, I kept stopping and starting over. I was used to people the size of Sofia, who was taller than me, but not ridiculously taller. Kristof was like a skyscraper, though; bringing my arm *down* at his head was impossible.

Anika Sensei was there, but she wasn't teaching, and Brandon Sensei didn't explain stuff as much as she did. Jenna and Julie Chung were there, too, but Jenna and I were only in the kids' class together for two months before she moved up, and Julie was older than Jenna. They were at least closer to my size, though. I tried to partner with them, but everything moved too fast, and they always seemed to pair up with black belts or each other.

Martha's mom had mediocre technique, but she was incredibly strong, so when she threw me, she *really* threw me.

A broad-shouldered blue belt named Miles almost elbowed me in the face while blocking punches. I kept standing the wrong way, doing elbow grabs instead of wrist grabs, and forgetting what to do with my arms.

It was a very long class.

At pickup time I bowed to Brandon Sensei (I was in nontalking mode so I couldn't thank him verbally), grabbed my stuff, and went out to the hallway to hug Dad.

"How'd it go?" he said.

I closed my eyes and breeeeeeeathed.

"Ah. It's okay, Stevie. You're okay. Let me talk to Sensei real quick and we'll go."

Dad's autistic like me, but he says he's neurotypical-passing (which means people can't tell he's autistic just by looking at him) because he's practiced so much. He smiled at me, eyebrows raised and lips together, as I leaned into him. I sat on the bench right outside the dojo as Anika Sensei came out and said hello.

I felt so thrashed that everything around me was a foggy blur, so I tucked my red belt into my bag and pulled out my new book. It was good to just read.

" . . ."

I didn't know how the author decided to combine figure skating and martial arts, but it was genius.

" . . . Stevie . . ."

I'd started the book at breakfast while Mom and Dad

talked about the usual stuff like politics and whether I should read during breakfast, and I was up to page 157.

"Stevie."

There was a light pressure on my shoulder. I looked up to see Dad's face.

"Dad. Read this." I held up *Peasprout Chen: Future Legend of Skate and Sword.* "It's awesome."

"I know, buddy. I gave it to you, remember? How about wearing your shoes?"

"The car's *right there,* Dad."

I could actually see it. Dad was parked right in front of the building, which used to be a warehouse but was now full of art studios, welders, and our dojo.

"City sidewalks, little man. There might be—"

"Broken glass, I know. And I'm not little. Or a man."

"Shoes, champ."

"Okay."

My pile of stuff slid onto the floor as I dug out my shoes. After carefully tying my shoelaces (it's important to get the double knots equal on both sides), I put everything into a new pile, this time in my arms. I nodded at Dad over the pile, and he chuckled. It was our usual post-aikido routine, and it would have felt good if class hadn't felt so bad.

✦ ✦ ✦

"Will they kick me out of the dojo if I quit the teen and adult class?"

That got Mom and Dad's attention.

"Whoa, hold on," Mom said from across the dinner table.

"Who's kicking who out of what?" Dad said through a mouthful of duck. Roasted duck legs are his specialty— he's ridiculously proud of them.

"Don't talk with your mouth full, Dad."

"Back up, Stevie," Mom said. "You haven't said anything about the class. What happened?"

"It was . . . hard. Different."

"Makes sense," Dad said, stabbing a piece of broccoli with his fork. "Big changes are hard."

"I'm sorry," Mom said. "What parts were hard?"

"All of them."

"Well. That narrows it down."

"What does Brandon Sensei do differently?" Dad said.

"Everything." I picked up my drumstick, looked at it, and put it down. I suddenly felt shaky, mad, exhausted, and frazzled, all at once.

"Everything's so *fast!*" I pulled my legs onto my chair, put my elbows on my knees, and grabbed my head. "The warm-ups are out of order, my friends aren't there, everyone's huge. . . ."

The chair felt too small, so I threw myself onto the couch

instead. A pillow fell onto my head, and I clamped it over my mouth and screamed into it. Screaming into pillows helps when I'm feeling overwhelmed, so I did it again.

Someone took a deep, loud breath and blew it out, but I couldn't tell if it was Mom or Dad. Maybe it was both. The couch cushion changed shape under me as Dad sat down.

"Foot massage?"

I moved the pillow enough to look at Dad and shake my head. He nodded and leaned back. Dad's good at foot massages and Mom's good at brushing my arms with her fingertips, but I just wanted them to sit with me.

"Honey, this is yours," Mom said.

"Ah, the SPLC *Intelligence Report*. Nothing says 'relaxation' like a bunch of articles about violent racists."

"Yes, more relaxation's the last thing we need around here," Mom said as she sat down on the other side of Dad.

"We could use more irony, though. Really low on irony."

"Stop fighting," I said.

Mom chuckled. "We're not fighting, honey."

"We're not? Wow, I'm totally misreading the situation."

"Dad. Stop."

I lay there listening to my heartbeat, the buzz of the refrigerator, the pillow fabric moving against my face, the upstairs neighbor's footsteps, and the occasional page being turned.

Eventually I dropped the pillow onto the floor.

"Better?" Mom reached over and squeezed my foot.

I shrugged.

"Interesting pitch on that first scream," Dad said. "Like an angry soprano."

That wasn't funny enough to make me smile, but it was better than Mom freaking out and Dad yelling at everyone, which is what used to happen when I had meltdowns. Dad would literally yell at everyone—me, Mom, the cat, people who put compostable items into the recycling bins—and Mom would bark about how acting like this wouldn't get me what I wanted, then storm out of the room. Then I was diagnosed as autistic, and then *Dad* was diagnosed, and they both started reading books about autistic rights and finally calmed the heck down.

"Can I stay in the kids' class?" I said.

"I think you're supposed to," Mom said.

"I mean, *only* the kids' class."

"Oh. I don't see any problem with that. Do you, honey?"

"Nope," Dad said. "You could try once more—the second time might feel better—but kids' class only is fine."

"Okay."

"I'm curious, though." Dad bent over and kissed my forehead. "Was there anything you liked?"

"Maybe Brandon Sensei."

"That's great!" Mom said. "What about him?"

"The way he moves."

"He *is* a sixth-degree black belt," Dad said.

"I also like that he's autistic."

"Me too." Dad got up, and my feet jostled a little as the couch cushion unsquished itself. "I'm listening, buddy. I just need some water."

"Did you like anything else?" Mom said.

"No."

It would be terrible to go back to the teen and adult class, but it'd be humiliating to tell people that I couldn't handle teen and adult class. And I actually wanted to keep going. How else would I get any better? But I didn't know if I wanted to go because I thought I *should* go, instead of wanting to go because I *wanted* to go.

Crying's awful—I hate the runny nose and the tears going down my shirt, and it makes me remember all the times I've been called a crybaby—but I started crying anyway.

"Hey, it's all right, sweetie." Mom scooted over and petted my head. "You don't have to put so much pressure on yourself."

In the kids' class I was awesome at aikido, but in the teen and adult class I was an out-of-place loser. It was like being in school. I didn't want aikido to feel like school.

It was a relief to go back to the kids' class, partly because Arthur was there. He was doing forward rolls when I got there, so I waited until he rolled to his feet and saw me before running to hug him. He hugged me back hard.

"You're home!" I let go and stuffed my shoes and bag into a cubby. "Finally!"

"I know, right?" Arthur giggled.

"How was the trip?" I said as we started our usual warm-up exercise, which was jumping as high as we could over and over. I let my arms flop all around, and Arthur swung his arms from side to side in front of his body.

"Remember my uncle who won't stop calling me Artie?"

"Yeah. So disrespectful." It's not Artie or Art—it's *Arthur*.

"Totally. My mom argued with him about it, and—"

He was interrupted by a squeal. A second later Martha barreled across the mats, and if Arthur hadn't stopped jumping, she'd have run him over like a freight train. They hugged instead.

"You guys can't start jumpy warm-ups without me!" Martha pretended to punch our shoulders.

"Yes, ma'am!" I saluted. "Private Steven Chang reporting for duty!"

"Private Arthur Levit reporting for duty, Admiral Bee!" Arthur started jumping again, and Martha immediately started, too. It took me a moment to figure out what was happening, so I waited for their second jump to join in. Martha likes to stretch her arms way over her head at the top of each jump. We laughed through seven or eight jumps, then threw ourselves on the mats to stretch. Anika Sensei came out of the women's and girls' changing room and smiled at us. I knew she was going to ask me about the teen and adult class, so I was relieved when Sofia and Malik started talking to her, even though I kind of hated that I was relieved.

Arthur's trip turned out to be incredibly boring. His favorite cousins got sick and stayed home, so he spent the whole week hanging around with grown-ups in restaurants or at his grandma's house.

"So? How was it?"

A classic Martha question—nothing about which "it" she meant. It's like she thinks I can read minds.

"How was what?"

"Sorry, how was the teen and adult class?"

"Uh . . . not great."

"Oh no," Arthur said. "Was it like when Kayleigh moved up?"

"What happened with Kayleigh?" Martha put her hands on her hips, which always looks funny when she's sitting down.

"Yeah, we haven't seen her since she stopped showing up."

Arthur sighed. "It'll be so nice when you two finally get phones. We texted after she stopped coming. She said she quit because teen and adult class wasn't any fun."

"It isn't," I said.

"You're different from Kayleigh," Martha said. "For her, 'not fun' probably just meant not being the best student in class anymore."

"How do you know?"

"It's obvious. Kayleigh was pretty stuck-up."

"Oh. Does that mean I'm stuck-up, too? Because seriously, it was like that for me, too."

"Stevie. That's not what I meant."

"Maybe I'm, you know, Kayleigh 2.0."

"No, you're not," Martha and Arthur said together. I couldn't help laughing.

"Can I convince you with a tackle-hug? I'd never tackle-hug Kayleigh!" Martha jumped up and spread her arms so wide that she almost fell over backward.

"Do you even know me?" I said, and we all laughed.

"Hello!"

Anika Sensei had made it across the dojo.

"Arthur, it's good to have you back!"

Arthur smiled with his whole face—seriously, every part of his face moved—and bowed. "Hai, Sensei. It's good to be back!"

"I love seeing you three together. It does my heart good. Can I borrow Stevie?"

"Hai, Sensei!"

"How did it feel being in the teen and adult class?"

Anika Sensei said after we'd sat in an empty corner of the dojo.

I slumped over.

"Hard."

She nodded. "I'm sure it did."

"Not just physically hard, either. It was *mentally* hard."

"Tell me more."

"Well . . . my friends weren't there. Everything happens differently. Everyone's bigger than me."

"True."

"Nobody really talks. I kind of like that part, actually, but . . ."

"But it's different."

"Yes. It's harder to know what the other person's doing. Sensei . . ."

"Yes?"

"Do I have to keep going to that class right now?"

Anika Sensei firmly shook her head.

"No. It's entirely up to you."

"But I have to move up permanently next year."

Anika Sensei made an upside-down U with her mouth, tilted her head, and looked off into space.

"Yes, but a lot will change before then. You did well in that class; next year you'll do even better. There's no rush."

"I did well? Really?"

"Yes. I could tell it was challenging, but you kept

going. The advanced students practically lined up to work with you."

"*Really?*"

"Really!"

"I couldn't tell!"

Anika Sensei smiled.

"Sometimes that's true for all of us. Excuse me, Stevie, I have to start class soon."

"Hai, Sensei. Thank you!"

Martha and Arthur waved me over to sit with them, and I realized how weird and lonely it'd felt to hunt for a space by myself in the other class. Could I get used to that until Martha and Arthur moved up? *If* they moved up? Yes. No. Maybe. I didn't know.

Sometimes figuring out what you really want to do is super hard.

One problem with so-called progressive parents (besides the fact that they call themselves "progressive" like my parents do) is they do terrible things like limit computer use to an hour per day. Martha's dads do it, too, and Arthur's parents have a zillion no-phone times, including meals, movie nights, and family meetings, which they always hold on Monday nights. That Monday Martha had to use her computer time to work on a school project, so instead of an hour-long chat with my best friends, I got emails. Short ones.

Good ones, though.

Remember Stella Jenkins? Forget Kayleigh, be like Stella.
—Arthur

I did remember Stella! When I was a white belt, she partnered with me a lot, she always said "hi," and she never got weird about it if I didn't make eye contact while talking. Stella moved up, but after she got her orange belt, she came back to be an attacker during my purple belt test. She only left Twin Rivers because her family moved to another state, where she was probably a blue belt by now.

Be like Stella.

Martha's email was even shorter.

Watch this. http://bit.ly/2nziBEO
—M

The link went to a video on a public TV website with a screen cap of Brandon Sensei throwing Kristof, but with different hair and a blue belt! The video's title was "Life on the Spectrum: Aikido."

Brandon Sensei had been on TV!

I clicked play, and the image dissolved to a shot of Brandon Sensei walking away from the camera as students trained around him. He gently raised and lowered his arms

like he was holding a bokken, and violins thrummed in the
background as he talked.

"Like many autistic people, I was bullied as a child.
I started learning aikido because I decided to make it stop."

Next he got attacked by everyone in the dojo but
calmly threw students in every direction, no matter how
fast they came at him. There was Kristof again, and Miles,
and Anika Sensei with a brown belt!

"But that's not why I stayed. I stayed because aikido
is . . . beautiful."

Next he threw a black belt I didn't know. His arms
made flowing circles as he threw her, and her whole body
spiraled in midair as she rolled. It looked like dancing, not
fighting.

"Being in the world is a high-intensity experience for
me—there's far too much stimulus to process at once."

For me, too.

"I have auditory hypersensitivity, so I hear . . . everything."

Yes!

"I'm very aware of the sensations within my body. Joints
moving, connective tissues stretching, muscles flexing

in exertion . . . I often feel like waves of vibration or electricity are moving through me."

Yes again!

"I can channel those internal experiences into aikido, which blends active physicality with psychological awareness in a way that's constantly challenging, but utterly natural."

The video ended with Brandon Sensei doing a perfect forward roll.

He was right. Aikido was beautiful.

I'd been so nervous at my first class, but Anika Sensei had said hello to me and Dad and hadn't cared that neither of us really looked her in the eye. She showed us how to do forward rolls, and it looked so cool, with her arms in a big curve and her head tucked in as she rolled. Everything was really hard at first, but everything also made sense. At school I have to do math problems the teacher's way even if there's a much easier way that works just as well, which makes no sense at all, but at the dojo we're always taught to do aikido in a way that works and feels good. It was pretty obvious that Anika Sensei and the other black belts really liked doing aikido together, even though they all did it kind of differently from each other.

Maybe that was why aikido was great. Doing aikido felt awesome, partly because you *have* to do aikido with other people. Mom and Dad say stuff to me like "We love you, beautiful boy" at random moments, and saying "I love you, beautiful aikido" would be the weirdest, most awkward thing a person could say in life, but it was kind of how I felt anyway. I *did* love aikido, it *was* beautiful, and Brandon Sensei felt the same way about it as I did.

I watched the video again, and again, and again, and again.

"You're sure about this?"

"No."

"There's no pressure, you know."

"I know."

"Nervous?"

"Dad. Of course."

Dad laughed.

"I admire your honesty."

"Mom says honesty is the best policy for ripping psychic Band-Aids off."

"I admire her honesty, too. Okay, big boy. I'll be right down the street. Can I hug you?"

"Yes."

We got out of the car and hugged.

"I'm so proud of you."

"Thanks, Dad."

"I love you."

"I love you, too."

As Dad drove off, I walked slowly into the warehouse. The dojo's regular door and big sliding door were both open, and I could see a slice of sunlight, white walls, and blue mats. There was a flash of movement as someone walked by, which was enough to trigger my overwhelmed thing where the whole world looks hazy and farther away than it really is.

Breathe.

I breathed deep into my belly, lowered my shoulders, and lifted my head. Brandon Sensei waved from the middle of the room as I entered. Nobody else was there yet.

"Stevie! Hello!"

"Hello, Sensei."

I bowed onto the mat and walked over to him.

"Sensei, can I ask a question?"

"Of course."

"Do you ever get mad at yourself for not being as good at aikido as you want to be?"

He nodded.

"I wouldn't say *mad,* but I've often felt . . . frustrated in that way, yes."

I looked up at the skylights. There was a fan in the ceiling right below each skylight; watching the fans turn helped me feel calm.

"I like your autism and aikido video."

"Thank you. Do you mean the 'Life on the Spectrum' video?"

"Yes, and I agree."

"About?"

"About aikido being beautiful."

"I'm so glad!"

I heard voices approach the doors behind me, then come inside.

"Ready to train?"

"Hai, Sensei."

Brandon Sensei nodded, and I turned, set my feet, and launched into a perfect forward roll.

Aikido. It's still the best thing ever.

A Girl's Best Friend

Cynthia Leitich Smith

I click my way from one furry face to the next, looking for a new best friend. The animal shelter website offers plenty of outstanding choices, all eager for forever homes.

A Chihuahua named Micky (male, two years, two months).

A bulldog named Benny (male, four years, zero months).

A German shepherd mix named Jazzy (female, two months).

A Labrador retriever mix named Snickerdoodle (female, three years, six months).

I hear Mama come in. "Sophie, baby, I'm back!"

Normally right now she'd be at rehearsal, singing and playing guitar with her rockabilly punk band, the Screaming Head Colds. That's why we moved to Austin—the live music capital of the world.

But Mama worked late today at her other job. She's a combo cook, maid, driver, and personal assistant to Miz Wilson, our landlady. In exchange, we get a serious break on rent. Our apartment is above Miz Wilson's detached garage. It's super small, but we love it. From here, we can walk to the public library, the lakefront, and the animal shelter. Mama says my school is one of the best in town.

Setting aside my tablet, I roll onto my tummy to peer through the wedge-shaped window at what we call "the big house" out front. It's a rainy June. Mama just finished planting daisies and marigolds in the flower boxes beneath the first-floor windows.

It could've waited until tomorrow morning, but Miz Wilson wanted it done today—period.

She's also the one who always says, "No pets allowed—period."

After her shower, I hear Mama's footsteps on the creaky hardwood floors of the living room below. Then I hear her climb the bolt-attached wooden ladder to my loft bedroom. "Sophie!"

She asks, "Are you fantasy shopping for dogs again?"

I flip over on my futon and hold up the image of Snickerdoodle on my tablet screen. "I know what our lease says, but how about I ask Miz Wilson to make an exception?"

Mama shakes her dark curls—the dyed faerie-blue

strand in front is clipped to one side. "Oh, honey, I don't think you should push it. We've got a sweet deal for this location."

I put on my pleading expression. For months, I've been begging Mama for permission to ask. She laughs. "Talk about puppy-dog eyes! Okay, but be respectful. And try not to get your hopes up. She's not what you'd call a flexible personality."

The big house was built in the 1920s and sits atop a high hill, overlooking the city and the state capitol. Like usual, Miz Wilson is perched at the wrought-iron table on the front terrace, drinking ice water and bird-watching.

"Is that a new tattoo on Dr. Ambrose's shoulder?" she mutters in the shade of the pecan tree. "I can't imagine how he expects his physics students to take him seriously."

I suspect Miz Wilson does more neighbor-watching than bird-watching.

I've already pulled up the animal shelter website and clicked through *Available Pets*.

"Excuse me, Miz Wilson?" I begin. "Mind if I have a word with you?"

"Did you bring the rent check?" she asks, lowering her binoculars. It's how she starts almost every conversation with me, no matter how many days until the money is due.

"No, ma'am," I reply, inching closer. "I've come to ask you an important question."

Miz Wilson is a handsome, freckled white lady with French tip fingernails. Her husband, Mr. Navarro, was Tejano, big in Democratic politics, and they used to host political action meetings in this house. They used to take long walks, hand in hand, through the neighborhood. They used to call each other "Precious." You'd never guess any of that, to know her now.

He died last year. Heart attack. Miz Wilson's three daughters had already moved far away—first for college, then for jobs and families of their own. Two of them got married here, though, and the receptions spilled out onto this terrace.

Mama says Miz Wilson is lonely.

I say it's harder to make friends when you're so thoroughly unpleasant.

"Please have a seat," she says. "Would you like a glass of water?"

She has strong opinions on what courtesy requires. And doesn't require.

I'm cautiously optimistic. We've had our share of chats. She's a little too nosy about my family, and I've had to explain more than once what it means that I'm a Muscogee-Osage girl and a Muscogee (Creek) Nation citizen.

But she did give Mama our bus fare to visit the branch

of family in Pawhuska, Oklahoma, last Christmas. Miz Wilson called it "a holiday bonus," adding, "I believe in fair pay for a job well done."

I sit and sip, quiet and still.

Miz Wilson doesn't like chatterboxes or fidgets.

I log back into my phone and put it down on the table so a pic of a dachshund named Sweet Potato (female, four years, seven months) smiles up at us. "She's the absolute cutest dog at the shelter," I begin. "I clicked through all two hundred and sixty-eight to make sure and—"

"Sophie Bigheart!" Miz Wilson exclaims. "What on earth is this? You know better!"

"I just thought I'd ask—"

"You thought wrong." Miz Wilson picks up the screen and gazes at Sweet Potato, and her expression briefly softens. "My husband, Charlie, and I used to have a wiener dog, back when our girls were young. Oh, how he doted on that animal!" Then she slaps my phone back down. "But your apartment is only four hundred square feet. There's no room for a dog. And rules are rules."

Mama was right.

Miz Wilson isn't what you'd call "a flexible personality."

While Mama and the Screaming Head Colds perform in town, I babysit little kids in the neighborhood. But we always make sure to reserve Monday nights for mother-daughter time.

This week, we're taking off work tomorrow, too, because it's my twelfth birthday.

Movie night starts in a few minutes. Up in my loft, I click through *New Arrivals*.

A boxer mix named Madeline (female, one year, seven months).

A collie mix named Frankie (male, nine months).

A terrier named Teacup (female, five years, four months).

A husky named Snowflake (female, three years, four months).

From downstairs, I can smell buttery popcorn. We plan to watch *Miss Congeniality* and *Miss Congeniality 2,* but first, a short film called *Red Earth Uprising* by a Choctaw filmmaker.

"Come on down, baby girl!" Mama calls. "It's showtime!"

"Coming!" I'm about to log out when . . . I can't help myself. I revisit the link labeled *Volunteer*. Again. I've had it bookmarked for over a week. I've read over the page at least twice a day.

Minimum age—12 years old.

"It's destiny," I tell myself.

"What's destiny?" Mama wants to know.

"Just a minute!" The shelter requires an orientation, a six-hour-a-month commitment, and a parent/guardian waiver, and that the same parent/guardian accompanies the young volunteer at all times. I scramble down the ladder to Mama, who's munching buttered popcorn on our love seat.

I say, "I'm ready to celebrate, and this year I know exactly what I want for my birthday."

As June melts into July, Mama and I complete our volunteer training and start walking shelter dogs on the hike-and-bike trail around the lake. We take them on field trips to our neighborhood, too.

Like usual, I ask for Sweet Potato. Like usual, somebody else has already taken her out for the day, but there are plenty of other pooches.

A poodle named Zsa Zsa (female, six years, one month). She dances a jig whenever anyone pays attention to her. What a cutie!

A Great Pyrenees named Giovanni (male, five years, one month). Such majesty, and he's enormous. The size of a miniature pony.

A Pomeranian mix named Sir Galahad (male, eight years, two months). Whip smart and high energy. He has lots to say, especially to the squirrels.

A rottweiler named Rye (male, four years, two months). A total sweetie! Never mind all the drool in his doggie kisses.

Day after day, dog after dog, in all their panting,

pooping, peeing, tail-wagging, "shake," "beg," "roll over" glory. "Good dog!" I praise every time we return one to the shelter.

Because it hurts less than saying "Goodbye."

"That's two!" Mama exclaims one morning as we climb the outdoor stairs to our apartment. "Rye and Zsa Zsa! Two dogs we've personally introduced to their future families."

Mama and I bump fists. Both sets of new owners adopted right away. Not everyone goes looking for a dog. Some folks meet one when they least expect it and fall in love.

"What's this?" There's a sheet of paper taped to our front door.

An eviction notice!

Mama tears it off and turns it over to read the handwritten note. "Miz Wilson claims that we've violated a clause of our rental agreement. She's terminating our lease!"

"Wait, what? What clause?" I want to know.

Shaking her head, Mama says, "No pets allowed. She must've spotted us walking one of the shelter dogs and thought it belonged to us, that we're hiding it here in the apartment."

✦ ✦ ✦

Come morning, I wake to Mama's muffled shouting. "You're being unreasonable! Open this door and *listen* to me!"

Peering out my window, I watch Mama pound three times on the double doors to the big house's kitchen. I glimpse Miz Wilson through the window inside. Then she disappears behind the blinds.

Mama pounds the door again. She tosses her hands into the air and stomps back toward the outdoor stairs to the apartment. Our door opens. Slams shut.

For a few moments, it's silent.

Then the microwave beeps and I hear the fierce strum of her guitar.

When I join her in the kitchen, Mama pauses her song. "Sorry if I woke you up."

"What happened?" I move to the counter, pick up a flour tortilla, and layer in black beans, turkey bacon, and shredded cheese. We usually have scrambled eggs.

Mama props her guitar alongside the doorframe. "Miz Wilson is the most pigheaded person I've ever met. She won't listen to reason. She refuses to speak to me at all. She's blocked my texts and says I'm no longer welcome in her home. She's demanded we pay our last month's rent and vacate the premises."

I open the refrigerator door to check—no eggs. "Should I start packing?"

"I've done some research." At the fold-out table, Mama

pours us each a glass of orange juice. "Tenants have rights. But we can't afford avocados, let alone a lawyer."

I reach for a second tortilla and make another breakfast taco, this one for my mother.

Once we start in on the dishes, Mama declares, "Sophie, I've had it! I'm not particularly fond of her highfalutin attitude on a good day, and now I can't very well imagine working for that woman after she's gone and accused us of being liars. After she's cut off *all* communication and wants to toss us out onto the street without even giving me a chance to tell her what's what."

Miz Wilson isn't the only one around here with a stubborn streak.

It's up to me to solve this predicament. I need a bigger power on my side.

Puppy-dog eyes.

That's the sunny day we finally get to walk Sweet Potato, who I nickname SP. She and I hit it off right away, like we've been best friends forever. I suggest to Mama that we treat her to a tour of our neighborhood. Sweet Potato promenades up the sidewalk alongside us, her short legs working double time.

That's when I spot the reflection off Miz Wilson's binoculars, pointed in our direction.

Right on schedule.

"I'll drop off the rent," I say, once we reach the long walkway up to the portico.

"Oh no, baby!" Mama crosses her arms. "You shouldn't have to face that grump."

"Not a problem," I reply. "I'll take Sweet Potato for protection."

Right then, Mama gets a phone call about that night's band gig.

I take advantage of the distraction to hightail it with SP up the concrete stairs.

At the terrace, Miz Wilson squares her thin shoulders. "Did you bring the rent check?"

"Yes, ma'am," I say, setting down the pup. "And I brought this thirsty dog, too. Her name is Sweet Potato, remember? From the shelter website?"

Tail flying every which way, the dachshund rushes over to charm her.

"I . . . I remember." Like it has a mind of its own, Miz Wilson's hand strokes the dog's smooth, short coat, gliding over droopy ears and a long body. A smile tugs at her lips, but she forces them back into a straight line. Miz Wilson adds, "But you shouldn't have brought all those dogs home. I simply can't go bending the rules, willy-nilly."

Jeepers. How many dogs does she think we have hidden in the apartment?

I set the rent check on the wrought-iron table.

Miz Wilson pours cool water into the spare tumbler and offers it to a grateful Sweet Potato.

"Mama and I didn't adopt *any* dogs." I pull up the shelter's volunteer page on my phone for Miz Wilson's inspection. "Look here. We're helpers. We *exercise* and *socialize* the dogs."

"You didn't bring home *any* dogs?" Miz Wilson asks, frowning at the screen.

"That's right," I assure her. "But I think Sweet Potato belongs here." I cross my fingers behind my back. "Not as a pet for me. A pet for you. This could be her forever home."

Her eyes light up, but . . . "D-dogs are expensive," Miz Wilson stammers. "They're a lot of work."

She has buckets of money and nothing better to do.

"I'll pay the adoption fee with babysitting money. I'll walk the dog and feed her and—"

"My pet, my responsibility," she replies.

"What if we walk the dog together?" I suggest. It's a risk. I bet she misses those long walks through the neighborhood with her late husband. But I'm not sure if the thought of having new, different company along the way will make her feel better or worse. On the other hand, anybody could tell she's been miserable. Maybe this will brighten her days and spirits. I have to try!

"We'd all walk together?" she asks. "The three of us?"

Is she blinking back a tear? "Yes, ma'am," I say.

"And you'll feed the dog?" she asks.

"Yes, ma'am," I say. "I can also teach her tricks."

Miz Wilson tucks in a full-blown smile. Her nod is all business. "I'd have to reimburse you for your time and efforts."

I try not to bounce in place. I try not to grin. "So, you're considering it?"

Miz Wilson picks up Sweet Potato and kisses her forehead. Then she tears the rent check to pieces. "I'd best reimburse you for all the pet care you'll be doing. Like I always say, I believe in fair pay for a job well done. Have your mother write me a new check for two-thirds of that amount."

So, that would be . . . what? *A third off the rent?* I was sure Mama would accept that as an apology.

Or at least the closest thing to one we were likely to get.

"What are you waiting for, Sophie Bigheart?" Miz Wilson adds. "Run down and tell your mother to get off the phone and bring my car around. I need to fill out the paperwork at the animal shelter. Just remember this here is my dog, not yours. I'll pay for her upkeep and vet bills."

Inside, I'm shouting: *A dog! A dog! A dog! A dog!* And such a happy-making, heart-healing dog, too. Just look at how she's charmed Miz Wilson. Out loud, I breathe, "Thank you."

"Nothing to thank me for." She's still petting SP, who's

181

soaking up the love. "You're the one who found my precious Sweet Potato."

That's a tone of voice I'm not used to hearing from Miz Wilson.

I'm so excited it's like glitter is falling all around us.

I'd better scoot before she changes her mind. But first I ask, "Uh, is it okay if I give you a hug?"

With a friendly wink, she replies, "Don't you dare."

Everly's
Otherworldly Dilemma

Ellen Oh

Sweat pooled underneath Everly Young's helmet before dripping down the back of her neck as she maneuvered her bike around the heavy pedestrian traffic outside the Heights Galleria Mall. She could hear her best friend, Max Bennett, cursing behind her. August in Washington, D.C., was never a pleasant affair. Especially when the tourists flooded the area.

"Flying monkey turds!" Max shouted when Everly braked suddenly for a quartet of mothers pushing their baby strollers. The women took up the entire sidewalk as they chatted together, ignoring the people trying to get around them.

"The Mommy Mafia are taking over the mall," Max said. "Don't try to get past them, or they'll slime you with baby vomit."

Everly groaned. "We only have a few weeks of summer left. And the movie starts in fifteen minutes. Why won't they move?"

"And I'm hungry," Max said.

"You're always hungry," Everly retorted.

Spotting a break in the stroller formation, Everly darted forward, eliciting a shout of anger from one of the moms. She could still hear the loud complaints as she raced ahead and pulled up to a partially full bike rack.

"Thanks a lot," Max groused as he locked up his bicycle next to hers. "How come I'm always the one that gets yelled at?"

"'Cause you're too slow." She slipped her messenger bag over her shoulder and hurried Max along, joining the eager throngs of people trying to enter the mall. Each turn of the revolving doors sent refreshing waves of cold air over them.

"Hurry up!" Everly fanned herself. "I'm melting."

When it was their turn, the two friends piled into the revolving door together and pushed their way into the bliss of air-conditioned paradise, only to find themselves jam-packed with even more people. Families with little kids, tourists with their big cameras, and groups of bored teens were everywhere.

"Great mounds of elephant dung balls! Now we don't have time to hit the food court before the movie," Max complained.

"That's okay, 'cause for some strange reason I'm not hungry," Everly said with a pointed look at Max. "I wonder why."

"Uh, sorry."

Everly shook her head in disgust. "What is it with you and poop?"

"It's a natural thing. Like gas. Everyone has it."

"Don't want to hear it."

"Like you don't do it . . ."

"Shut up."

The two friends bickered amicably as they shuffled along with the crowd and headed to the theater. After a short wait in the ticket line, they were heading to the concession stand to buy some popcorn, when Everly caught sight of something strange.

The short man with the pointy nose who had just snuck into Theater 4 was most definitely a goblin. His hat gave him away. Goblins had huge ears that they could never disguise, so they relied on hats and other articles of clothing to cover them up. This goblin was wearing a black woolen skullcap on a scorching-hot summer day. And given his stealthy movements, he was up to no good. But then again, goblins usually weren't.

A rush of adrenaline surged through Everly's body as she stared at the goblin. She tugged at Max's arm, causing half his popcorn to spill out.

"Turds on a stick! Look what you made me do." He glared at her, blowing at the blond swath of hair that always fell into his eyes. "Now I'm definitely not sharing."

"Forget the popcorn." Everly yanked on Max's shirt. "You have to follow me."

She headed down the hall and approached the double doors to Theater 4. Suddenly nervous, she clutched the messenger bag she always carried with her. She could do this. She could stop the goblin if he tried anything. With a deep breath, Everly reached for the door.

Before she could open it, Max pulled away and peered up at the small marquee sign above the doors. "Wait a minute! This is *The Return of Lolly and the Dandelion Gang*. That's a little-kid movie. We're supposed to see *Furiously Fast in Space*. Did you buy the wrong tickets?" He was digging his ticket out of his back pocket when Everly yanked the door open and shoved him in.

"What are you doing?" Max whispered loudly.

"We're hunting," Everly replied. Her eyes scanned the crowd for the goblin, while her ears were assaulted by the lollipop music from the large dancing possum on the screen.

"Do we have to right now? In here of all places? You know I hate that rat. Used to scare me to death when we were little."

"It's a possum," Everly hissed.

Max looked up at the screen and shuddered. "It still scares me. That's it. I'm getting out of here."

He turned toward the door but stopped as Everly grabbed his skinny arm with a vise-like grip. Max flailed around a bit but succumbed to her greater strength. Everly had always been bigger than him.

"One day I'm gonna hit my growth spurt and I'll be taller than you, just you wait," he said.

"Stop being a baby, or I'll tickle you." Everly and Max had been friends for over ten years, and she knew exactly where to poke and tickle him for maximum irritation. Plus, if she tickled Max too hard, he always peed his pants.

The threat silenced him. Everly maneuvered Max into the empty back row and forced him to sit next to her as she scanned every corner of the theater.

Max cursed under his breath.

"Watch it! There are little kids all around us," Everly said.

"Yeah, well, it's your fault if they hear me. I shouldn't even be watching a dancing rat in a tutu . . ."

"Possum."

". . . and its stupid gang of pukey giggling flowers. Man, I hate that rat. . . ."

Just then, Everly caught sight of the goblin and covered Max's mouth.

"Shhhhhh, right there, see him?" she asked, pointing

at the short man who was fixated on a small family seated a few rows ahead of him.

Max peered over, only to lurch back in horror.

"That's a goblin! And a nasty-looking one, too."

Everly nodded grimly. "And I think he just found a perfect target." She pointed to a woman who was cradling a crying baby in one arm and trying to pass small cups of popcorn to her two other young children. Her little girl kept sneaking out of her seat and into the aisle so she could dance along with the music, her eyes locked on the screen.

Suddenly the baby started wailing. The mother tried to soothe it, but the cries grew louder, disrupting the viewers around them.

"Don't do it, don't do it," Everly muttered under her breath. "Aw, come on, lady. Don't leave those kids alone."

"She's totally gonna do it," Max muttered back.

They watched as the mother said something to her oldest child. She pulled her young daughter back into her seat, and then left the theater with the crying baby.

"She did it," Max said.

They shared a quick look of worry.

"Don't take your eyes off those kids," Everly warned. Nervousness filled her stomach. She knew by the churning of her gut that the goblin was targeting this little girl.

She slipped her hand into her messenger bag and gripped the handle of the torch that Max's dads had given her. The torch was supposedly the world's brightest flashlight, powerful enough to burn a hole through her bag in a minute. It was just the right tool for fighting goblins.

Everly was six when she found out Max and his family were not human. Max was a shape-shifter, and his two dads were vegetarian werewolves. Everly thought it was the coolest thing in the world. She'd always adored fairy tales, and she'd wanted to believe they were true. When Max's dads, Adam and Jeff Bennett, realized Everly could see through the masks of the Otherworldly, they taught her how to protect herself, specifically from the Buraku, which are Otherworldly that are considered dangerous. There was salt to repel magical creatures with evil intentions; a flashlight for goblins, imps, ghouls, and any folk who couldn't bear the light of the sun; and silver or iron to drive them all away.

With her flashlight, Everly felt confident about tackling an evil goblin.

Well, sort of. Truth was, she'd never had to drive an evil Otherworldly away. Most of the magical creatures she knew were her friends. But this goblin was up to no good. Her churning stomach affirmed it.

Everly took several calming breaths, willing herself to get up and approach the goblin. Maybe he was a vegetarian goblin who was only in the theater to watch the Lolly movie because he was a big fan of possums. Maybe he was only staring at the little girl because she was such a good dancer, and not because she looked delicious. Sweat dotted her forehead. No excuses. She had to get rid of the goblin.

Just as Everly was planning her approach, the little girl jumped out of her seat and began dancing again in the aisle. Her older brother was paying no attention to her; he was too busy laughing at the impossible gymnastics of the large possum, who was dancing, singing, and playing the banjo on the big screen.

The goblin rose and approached stealthily. Everly jumped to her feet. There was no time to plan. She had to stop him!

"Flying monkey turds!" Max shouted. There were frowns, and one mother loudly shushed them. Everly used the distraction to plop the little girl back into her seat. From her bag, she grabbed her torch, and was about to use it on the goblin when he disappeared.

Everly turned to Max. "You stay here and make sure that the goblin doesn't come back for her."

"Wait, Everly!" Max said, but she was gone.

Goblins had the ability to teleport short distances. She scoured the hallway and caught sight of the slight swing of a nearby door. She tore through it and entered a dark, narrow hallway. Everly switched on her powerful flashlight and pointed it at the goblin. He shrieked frantically, covering his eyes.

"What do you propose to do with me?" The goblin's voice was sharp and high.

That was a really good question. Everly was only trying to stop the goblin from taking the girl. She hadn't thought beyond that.

"You need to leave and never come back! If I ever catch you here again, you're gonna be so sorry!" Everly said with more confidence than she really had, which was none at the moment.

"Sorry? Worthless human. You have no power over me! You're a mere mortal." The goblin sneered, but his hands still covered his eyes.

He surged forward, knocking Everly onto the floor. Her flashlight rolled into the corner. The goblin crowed as he wrapped his cold, spindly hands around Everly's foot and dragged her toward him. She kicked at him wildly, connecting with his nose. *Snap!* He let out a keening sound of pain.

Everly reached for her horseshoe magnet and stabbed the prongs into the goblin's face. He gave a terrifying shriek and released her, steam rising from the two square marks on his cheek. Everly dropped the magnet into her bag and retrieved the torch. Then she scrambled to her feet. As she ran for the door, she pulled out a large container of sea salt.

"Foul human!" the goblin shouted. He jumped up and charged after her.

She could smell his rancid breath. Tucking the torch under her arm, she shook a handful of sea salt into her hand and threw it at the goblin, just as his clawlike fingers raked through her ponytail. The goblin fell away, yelping, the illusion of his human visage completely stripped away. Everly could now see his true form—pale gray, wrinkled skin covering a misshapen body and a gruesome face that was all sharp teeth and pointed features.

Unnerved, Everly was backing toward the door when a silver net flew past her and dropped onto the goblin. It immediately tightened over the creature, immobilizing him.

Everly whirled around and caught sight of two tall teenagers wearing forest green uniforms. One was a beautiful girl in rich shades of brown—dark brown hair, light brown skin, and medium brown eyes. She stood next to a tall, handsome redheaded boy with brown eyes. He held a golden trident in his right hand, and chains of the same silver netting wrapped diagonally across his torso. Golden rune symbols were embroidered on their left breast pockets. For the first time since chasing the goblin, Everly felt cold fear in the pit of her stomach. They were Shinobi Rangers, responsible for patrolling the Owari Gate, the only access point between their world and the Otherworld.

Her eyes darted to the empty hallway behind the Rangers. If Max came back, he'd be in terrible danger.

The Rangers stared down at the goblin, who was still shrieking. The girl spoke first.

"The salt and flashlight were smart. But it was foolish of you to tackle a goblin alone. Especially this one."

The goblin finally went silent.

"We've been following this scum for days now. You're lucky to be alive."

Redhead pointed his trident at the goblin. A shining light gleamed from its three tips, surrounding the frightened creature.

"What are you doing?" Everly yelled.

The light intensified all around the goblin. Moments later, he was gone.

"Did you kill him?" Everly asked.

The older girl shook her head. "No, unfortunately. He has to go to trial first. We sent him directly to prison."

Everly was relieved. Even though the goblin was evil and had tried to kidnap a child, she didn't want anyone killed. Just the idea of it made her queasy.

"Tell me, how long have you been able to see the Otherworldly?" the girl asked.

"Otherworldly?" Everly played dumb.

"We police the Owari Gate between our worlds vigilantly, but some scum, like that goblin, find a way to sneak in. Normal people can't see them. But you can, right?"

Everly nodded cautiously.

"What have your dealings been with them?" the boy asked in a clipped voice. "Are they your friends?"

"No! They usually run away from me. . . ."

"You're lucky," he said. "You could have been kidnapped or worse."

Everly shrugged. "They seemed harmless, but some really scare me."

The Ranger glared at her. "You are dead wrong. They should all scare you."

Everly jutted her chin. "You're kind of scary, too," she said, then asked, "Are *you* an Otherworldly?"

The Ranger's glare turned icy-cold. "I'm nothing like them. I'm human. Cameron Morrison, captain of the Shinobi Rangers."

"Wow. You seem awfully young to be a captain. . . ."

The Ranger smirked. "You know nothing! Correction, you know a little something, but nothing truly important, which makes you a danger to yourself and others."

The other Ranger laughed at his words. Everly fought back her temper. "I was just curious because you are using magic. . . ."

"Just because I'm utilizing magical weapons does not mean I'm using magic," Ranger Morrison retorted.

Everly's mouth formed into an O at his jerky attitude. "Er, sorry. I didn't mean to offend." She began to inch toward the door, desperately wanting to get away from them.

Before Everly could make a run for it, though, the Ranger plucked the flashlight from her hand.

"Hey, that's mine! Give it back!"

Cameron asked, "How does someone who has never dealt with the Otherworldly know how to use salt, iron, and a powerful flashlight?"

Everly's brain froze, her tongue heavy and thick in her mouth. Staring at his cold dark eyes, Everly got the chills. He wouldn't hesitate to use his trident on Max and his dads.

"The internet, duh!" She scowled. "If you saw weird, creepy things that no one else could see, wouldn't you research it online to make sure you could protect yourself?"

The girl Ranger chuckled. "I like you. I'm Darcy Watson, and I think you're going to be a real asset."

"Asset to what?"

"The Ranger cadet program."

"Huh?" Everly could feel her mouth gaping again. Forcing it shut, she looked at the two Rangers with a wary gaze. This was not good. She wasn't supposed to catch their notice. The Rangers were just as much the enemy as the goblin was. She wondered how she could get away without making them suspicious.

"Goblins are sneaky and dangerous," Darcy said. "But you were able to follow him and immobilize him, at least for a little while. You're brave, if a bit reckless, and definitely cadet material."

Darcy's words made her extremely nervous. Before she

could thank her, Cameron interrupted. "Don't be so sure. There's a fine line between reckless and stupid. I don't think she's Ranger material."

A fierce anger rose up Everly's chest, burning her throat. That was the last straw!

"You don't know anything about me!" she spit out. "You think you're better than me, but you're not! You're just a know-it-all teenage loser. I didn't ask for your help, so why don't you just leave me alone?"

Darcy raised her hands to placate her. "He doesn't mean any disrespect. He's just suspicious of everyone. He doesn't even trust his own grandmother."

With a snort, Everly began to walk away, but Darcy stepped in front of her.

"Look, what we should have told you from the start is that anyone who has the sight has to be recruited into the cadets, because we need them," she said. "Rangers don't last past the age of eighteen, when we lose our sight. We need to recruit any potential Ranger to our cadet program."

"Thanks but no thanks," Everly said, still angry with Cameron. "It's not like my parents are going to let me join anyway."

Cameron humphed. "Let her go," he said. "Told you she's not cadet material. She doesn't have what it takes."

"What's that? Being a humongous jerk?"

Cameron gave Everly a disgusted look, but Darcy cut him off before he could speak.

"Everly, don't listen to him. This is about keeping people safe. You *do* care about your family and friends, don't you?"

A chill went through her at Darcy's words. "Of course!" Everly said. That was the problem. She was very worried for her friends.

"Join the cadet program and fight for our human right to live free of dangerous Otherworldly creatures," Darcy said.

"But I'm only twelve," Everly protested.

Darcy exchanged amused glances with Cameron.

"I was nine and Darcy was ten when we joined," he said. "We knew it was our duty, and we were proud to do it. Not to join would have been unpatriotic." He paused for a moment, looking her over. "But you probably don't care about things like patriotism and civic duty."

At that moment, Everly would have given anything to have the magical ability to turn Cameron into a cockroach and stomp on him. Instead, she said, "I. Don't. Like. You."

"Listen, don't let him get to you," Darcy said. "I promise the rest of us aren't like him. Why don't you come to headquarters tomorrow and meet the others and the chief? You need to do that before making any decision."

Everly wanted to say no. She knew she should say no.

But something about the condescending smirk on the older boy's face made her want to prove him wrong.

Darcy held up her hand and showed Everly her large pearl ring.

"If you're a cadet, you get to try out the magical weapons in our arsenal and find the one that suits you best," Darcy said. She aimed the pearl at the far wall, and it released a pure white light that was more powerful than Everly's torch.

Darcy smiled at the wonder and longing on Everly's face. "So what do you say?"

Everly didn't respond right away. Her eyes drifted from the magic pearl to the golden trident and the silver netting. To be able to use magical weapons would almost be like having magic, she thought.

"I have kendo on Saturday mornings, but I'm free all afternoon," Everly said slowly.

Darcy smiled in relief. "Great! Meet me in front of the theater at one p.m. tomorrow. I'll take you to headquarters myself."

"Fine, but I don't want him coming!" Everly pointed at Cameron.

Cameron smirked back at her. "As you wish." He banged his trident on the ground. Cameron and Darcy vanished as quickly as they had appeared.

Even though the mom and her baby had returned, Max was still watching out for the kids in the possum movie.

Everly filled him in. Horrified, Max insisted that they go and tell his dads right away.

Being next-door neighbors with her best friend had always been really convenient for Everly. Since her parents were high-ranking federal officials who were always working, Max's house was Everly's second home.

Walking into Max's living room, she saw a familiar scene. Adam, Max's accountant father, was arguing with Marie in the living room, while Jeff, the artist, was in the kitchen making dinner.

Marie was a real-life fairy, and also Max's godmother. His fairy godmother. Everly always had to chew her lip to stop from laughing about that fact. But it gave her great joy to call Max Cinderella whenever he got on her nerves.

"We have a problem," Max announced ominously. "Everly was contacted by Shinobi Rangers."

The adults all gasped in horror.

"Give us the details, Everly," the fairy said. "Don't leave anything out."

Taking a deep breath, Everly launched into the events of the day. When she was done, the house was absolutely quiet, except for the crunching of Max's potato chips.

Adam let out a heavy sigh. "You'll have to avoid the mall for a while."

"No, she has to go," Marie interjected. "This is exactly what we need."

"You can't be serious! It's not safe."

"You underestimate her abilities."

"No, *you* underestimate the depth of Shinobi prejudice!"

"Adam, times are changing," said Marie.

"Not for us," Adam said. "You're a fairy, so it's different for you."

"No. I've been discriminated against, too!"

In the blink of an eye, Adam's smooth blond looks shifted to those of a snarling werewolf. His pretty blue eyes turned blood-red, and his lips retracted to show a fearsome array of sharp, elongated canines.

"Don't you dare, Marie! Don't try to compare your experience to ours. You left the fairy court because you befriended the Buraku. That's not the same. You can never know what it feels like to be one of us, feared and despised by all."

She made an impatient sound. "You know as well as I do that the Shinobi do not differentiate among the Otherworldly. They will hunt down a rogue fairy no differently than a rogue Buraku."

Adam's werewolf face receded.

"You're so naive! A fairy is not the enemy until they turn. But the Buraku are always the hunted, even if we've never harmed anyone in our lives. Not just by the Shinobi, but by King Magnus and the fairy army and our own fellow citizens. It is how things have always been. It's why we left the Otherworld."

"But if things don't change, this world will be no different," she said sharply.

Both Adam and Jeff looked horrified.

"Don't tell me you had a vision?" Jeff asked.

She nodded. "War is coming. I've seen it. And this time, it will not be contained to the Otherworld."

"What do you mean, Aunt Marie?" asked Everly.

"During the First War, the Shinobi Rangers and the fairy army kept the fighting from entering the human world," Max said.

"Well, that's the official version," the fairy said. "And that's why we are in trouble. Modern rangers have been taught to hunt the Buraku. But they and humans don't realize that the fairy folk are their real enemies. We must prepare for war."

"How?" Jeff asked in a despairing voice. "Last time, an army of samurai warriors protected the gate. Now the Rangers are just a bunch of kids who chase down stray Buraku. They aren't ready for this."

"And that's where Everly comes in," said Marie, turning to Everly. "You can join the cadet program and help unite the Rangers and the Buraku."

Everly asked, "I've been told over and over again how important it is to avoid the Rangers. Why are you telling me to become one?"

"This isn't a good idea. If the Rangers investigate her, they'll find all of us," Adam said.

"It's a risk," Marie admitted. "But there is no other choice."

"I don't know, Aunt Marie." Everly was shaking her head in dismay. "I'm not sure I can help."

The fairy floated to Everly and grabbed her hands. "But will you try?"

"Of course," Everly said.

Marie's smile was brilliant. "Then I have something for you."

She held up a small purple stone, decorated with a beautiful pattern of golden runes.

"This is a magic fairy stone," she said. "If you accept it, magic will begin to grow inside of you."

"You have no right to do this," Adam protested.

"This is Everly's choice," said Marie.

"She's just a kid," Jeff chimed in.

"If war comes, being a child will not protect her."

The two werewolves subsided.

"What will happen to us?" Everly asked.

"Magnus, the fairy king, would enslave the human race while trying to annihilate the Buraku. We are all in danger." The fairy paused.

"But in my vision, I saw you, Everly."

Everly blinked in surprise. "Me? What was I doing?"

"You were dressed like a Ranger and leading an army of Buraku. It will be perilous. The outcome is uncertain.

But seeing you gave me a sense of hope. So I ask you again: Will you try to help us?"

"Yes, I will," Everly responded firmly.

Marie smiled and handed Everly the stone. Suddenly the room faded away, along with Max and his two fathers. The pale blue walls of the Bennett house disappeared, and the Persian rug morphed into thick, tall grass.

Everly felt the cool night breeze blow through her ponytail. Everly and Marie were in a forest, standing within a ring of stones and wildflowers. A full moon shone brightly in a star-filled sky, bathing the area in soft light. The grass tickled Everly's bare feet. She could smell honeysuckle and pine trees. A hard shiver slid down her spine as she stared at the dark forest surrounding them.

"Where are we?" Everly asked.

"We are in the dream woods of the Otherworld," said Marie. "Only our spirits are here; our bodies are still back at Max's house."

"So I'm dreaming?"

"More like a waking dream," the fairy responded.

"But why am I here?"

"My dear child, what I'm asking of you will be dangerous. I can't ask you to do it defenseless. That is why I'm going to give you a choice," Marie said. She looked at the stone in Everly's hand and traced a delicate finger over the symbols on it. "These are runes: Ansuz Eihwaz

Algiz. They represent good fortune, protection, and defense. Rune magic is ancient and powerful. I don't know what powers the rune stone will give you, because everyone is different. But I know that with this stone, and your training in the use of magical weaponry, you will become the greatest and most powerful Ranger.

"Before you accept, though, you must make a choice. Magic is a powerful responsibility. If you willingly accept it, you will become a defender of the Otherworldly. You will become, in part, one of those hunted by the very people you are planning to join. Once you accept, you can never undo it, even if you come to hate it."

"Why would I hate it? I have always wanted to have magic," said Everly, excitement rising within her. This was a dream come true.

"Let me show you why," the fairy said, right before she disappeared along with the purple stone.

The light dimmed, and the heaviness of the night pressed against Everly's flesh. Her eyes darted to the dark forest. A dreadful sound filled her ears. Something was moving in the shadows. Something big and hulking. The putrid smell of death and decay struck her, and her eyes widened with horror at the sight.

A gigantic troll lumbered toward her.

"Aunt Marie! Where are you?" Everly shouted.

Her heart hammered as she stared in dismay at the troll.

Its skin was gray and filthy. She could see the sharp, jagged teeth in its wide crevice of a mouth as it grunted at her. It stood just outside the fairy circle, drool running down its craggy jaw, its massive hands extended toward her. But it stepped no further.

Everly realized it couldn't cross the ring of stones surrounding her. Just as she began to breathe again, the hairs on the back of her neck stood on end, making her pivot. She screamed in terror as a bevy of supernatural creatures came at her. Full-on werewolves that were nothing like Jeff and Adam bared their fearsome fangs, followed by goblins, kappas, fox demons, centaurs, ogres, witches, and vampires.

They stood around the edge of the fairy circle, watching her. Everly didn't know what they wanted. She didn't know what she was supposed to do. They were frightening. She closed her eyes and remembered what Adam had just said. *The Buraku are always the hunted.*

Everly took a deep breath. How was she to know who was safe and who would see her as a meal? This wasn't the same as the goblin situation, where she knew he was up to no good. She opened her eyes and noticed how patient and quiet they were. No gnashing of their teeth, no grunting or shrieking or howling. Even the troll stood quietly, shifting his weight from one foot to the other. What were they waiting for? What did they want?

Everly remembered the Buraku greeting of protection that Jeff had taught her. She slowly turned in a circle, catching the gaze of every creature before her, and bowed. "Peace to you, my brothers and sisters. I mean you no harm."

There was a moment of utter stillness before all the Buraku bowed in return. But still, they waited. Everly realized she couldn't stay in the circle all night. If they meant her no harm, then she had to trust them. She had to step out of the protective circle. Everly held a hand to her rapidly beating heart.

She stepped out.

Immediately the Buraku moved aside and lined up to form a path. Everly bowed again and walked past them until she reached a large rock, where the purple rune stone sparkled. When she turned around, the Buraku had vanished. She was alone.

"Marie? Are you here?" Everly yelled. The night was quiet all around her.

Everly stared at the stone, hearing the fairy's words again.

Once you accept it, you can never undo it.

Everly had always wanted magic, but now that the offer was before her, she didn't know if it was the right thing to do. But she thought of Max and Jeff and Adam. She thought of how they'd had to escape from the Otherworld because they were hunted by the fairy folk. If war came to her home, then none of them would ever be safe again. She would never forgive herself if something happened to her friends and her family. Plus, just how powerful could she be with magic?

She picked up the stone, it began to warm, and the symbols seemed to glow from within.

Everly looked around. What was she supposed to do now? She pressed the stone to her chest just as it flashed a hot, bright light. She felt a sharp, stinging pain, and then the heat was burning from within, as if she were being consumed alive. It was so hot, she wanted to rip her clothing off. She would have screamed, but she was paralyzed.

Just as she thought she'd made a horrifying mistake, the fire went out and she was back in Max's house, lying on the floor with everyone staring at her.

"Ow," she said. A huge billowing cloud of smoke blew out of her mouth.

Marie grinned like a Cheshire cat. "Welcome, hero of the Buraku!"

Everly didn't feel like a hero, but staring at the worried faces of her friends, she knew she would do anything to protect them. Even if it meant leading an army into battle. A thought struck her.

"Aunt Marie, was I carrying a weapon in your vision?"

She nodded.

"Cool," said Everly. "I'm so ready."

Reina Madrid

R. J. Palacio

1.

Reina wasn't her real name. Maria Eugenia was. But when Maria Eugenia Madrid first moved to the neighborhood at the age of six, none of the other kids could pronounce the new girl's name the way her mother pronounced it (as one long word with a series of uncertain vowel sounds in the middle). *Mah-ree-ah-ew-hen-ee-ah*. Instead, the neighborhood kids found it much easier to call Maria Eugenia by the other name Mrs. Madrid used for her daughter: Reina. *Ray-nah*. That was simpler to pronounce. The neighborhood kids didn't know that it meant "queen" in Spanish. They didn't know that Mr. Madrid, who had tragically died only four months before mother and daughter had moved here, used to call her that, too. (Actually, Mr. Madrid's pet name for Maria Eugenia was Reinita, which meant "little queen.") But the neighborhood kids didn't know or care about any of that. All they knew or cared about was that (a) Reina Madrid could run as fast as all the boys on 160th Street (except for Roy Ponte, but nobody could run faster than Roy) and (b) Reina Madrid was an excellent kickball player. This might or might not have had to do with all the weekends she spent playing *fútbol* with her father when she was little. All anyone knew was that when it was Reina Madrid's turn to kick, tiny as she was, everyone in the infield took three steps back.

The kids from the neighborhood played kickball in the courtyard behind the three buildings that faced the avenue. There was a strip of grass that spanned the length of the buildings, just wide enough for bases, and that was where all the kids congregated. The apartment complex itself was quite lovely: small, Tudor-style, four-story buildings, with pretty gardens in front of each one. It was these gardens that had compelled Mrs. Madrid to rent the apartment on 160th Street, even though it was out of her price range. When she had started looking for rentals, the Realtor had only initially shown her apartments around Seventy-Fourth Street, under the subway overpass. This, he reasoned, was where she should live because it was a predominantly Spanish-speaking neighborhood.

"You'll be comfortable here," he assured her.

Mrs. Madrid, however, who had left a life of true comfort in her native country to come to New York while her husband pursued his graduate degree, found the constant thunder of the subway overpass and the treeless streets on Seventy-Fourth Street depressing. Nor did she like the Realtor's insinuation, one she had found among her husband's North American friends, that just because she came from one South American country, she automatically had much in common with people from other South American countries.

"Each country is different," she would try to tell them. "Each country has its own history and culture and tastes."

So when the Realtor kept showing her rentals in the same treeless neighborhood, she insisted, in her thickly accented English, that he show her other neighborhoods—preferably ones with "very big trees."

Reina was in the car when the Realtor drove them to the new listing on 160th Street. The avenues here were lined on both sides with enormous elms and sycamores and, on the corner of 162nd, flanked by two ancient weeping willows that arched over the street like a billowy gate, marking the entrance to the neighborhood. Her mother commented that the trees here reminded her of the flame trees along the beautiful boulevards of her homeland. The Realtor made a face, obviously misunderstanding her.

"No, no, Mrs. Madrid!" he said, trying nevertheless to remain polite. "There aren't many fires here, no."

"What my mother is saying is that these trees remind her of the trees where she comes from, which are called flame trees," Reina interjected.

Even at six, she was already used to acting as an interpreter for her mother's broken English.

"Ohh!" said the Realtor, still not quite understanding, but by then he had pulled up to the building on 160th Street, and Mrs. Madrid, seeing the well-appointed gardens in front, announced happily: "This is it! We will take this apartment!"

"But this building is out of your price range, Mrs. Madrid," said Mr. Damper.

"Dile á Mr. Damper due no me importa," she told me.

"She says she doesn't care," Reina said to him.

"And the apartment is on the fourth floor, the top floor," he said, trotting behind Mrs. Madrid. "You had said you didn't want anything above the second story."

By then, Mrs. Madrid had walked to the front of the building and was taking it all in with an air of satisfaction, as if looking at a scene she recognized from a once-forgotten dream.

"Dile que éste es el apartamento que quiero," she told Reina firmly with a flick of her hand.

"She says this is the apartment she wants," Reina said, skipping behind her mother.

By then Mr. Damper had given up trying to talk directly to Mrs. Madrid, and turned to Reina.

"Tell her there are no other Spanish people in this neighborhood," he said, his eyes opened wide as if he was saying something of the utmost importance.

Mrs. Madrid turned to look at him. She wore thick glasses with green frames that curved upward at the sides like the tails of the Cadillac she had just sold to pay for their moving expenses. She was a petite woman, very elegant in her white gloves, very beautiful.

"This is the apartment I want, Mr. Damper," she said with a smile, enunciating every word so that there could be absolutely no misunderstanding her.

2.

It didn't take Reina long to become one of the pack of neighborhood kids. In Queens, in those days (the 1970s), your neighborhood was strictly limited to a one- or two-block radius. The kids on 160th Street, for instance, were a whole different set of kids from the ones on 158th or 162nd Street. There was no firm rule about it, but groups rarely mingled. The only exception was the building at the very end of 158th Street. This was where Franny Jones lived in apartment 2D. Franny was Reina's best friend.

They had met on Reina's third day in the neighborhood.

Reina was sitting on the front stoop of her building with her mother, waiting for the super to come to fix their stove. Franny and her older sister, Carol, were playing with the group of then unfamiliar kids in the long, grassy courtyard behind the buildings. Reina sat very close to Mrs. Madrid, pretending not to notice the kids and ignoring her mother's entreaties to join them. It was only when a bright pink Spalding ball bounced in front of them, and Reina was forced to catch it so it wouldn't hit her in the face, that she reluctantly acknowledged the group of kids by throwing the errant ball back to them. It was a good, strong throw coming from a six-year-old. The other kids, who ranged in age from six to nine, might have asked her to join them at that moment, but she quickly went back to pretending they didn't exist and sidled even closer to her mother. At moments like this, Reina wanted to be like a tattoo on her mother's arm. This was how shy she was around children she didn't know.

The super arrived just as the kids were dispersing. It was dinnertime. The moms were calling their kids in from their various windows along the long courtyard. Franny started walking toward the avenue with Carol, but stopped in front of the stoop as Mrs. Madrid was trying to explain to the super that the stove in the apartment would not turn on. Reina pretended not to see Franny lingering near the stoop, eavesdropping.

"My mom says the stove won't turn on," Reina said to

the super. Ironically, she was not the least bit shy around adults.

"Have you turned on the pilot light?" the super asked.

"I don't understand," Mrs. Madrid kept saying. "Pilot?"

"We don't know what you mean," Reina explained.

"The pilot light! The pilot light!" the super answered impatiently, before storming into the building and up the stairs to their apartment. Mrs. Madrid followed quickly, and Reina was about to follow, when Franny spoke to her for the first time.

"Your mother looks like Maria in *West Side Story*," she said flatly, as if she were stating the time.

"What?" said Reina.

"Maria in *West Side Story*!" Franny repeated.

"What's *West Side Story*?"

"You never saw *West Side Story*?"

"Reina!" Mrs. Madrid's voice echoed down the stairwell. *"Ven para traducir!"*

"Is that your name? Ray-na?" said Franny. She had an imperious air about her, like she wasn't used to being disobeyed. She had green eyes and sandy-brown hair and freckles.

"No, it's *Mah-ree-ah-ew-hen-ee-ah*," answered Reina.

"Mah-ree-what?" said Franny, somewhat disapprovingly.

"Reina!" her mother called again.

"I gotta go," said Reina.

"I'm Franny. You throw good. I'll call for you tomorrow and you can play with us."

"Okay, bye."

"Bye, Reina!"

Reina dashed up the stairs, two at a time. She had never heard the term "call for you" before but intuited that it meant she had a new friend. Exhilarated, but still nervous, she got to the apartment just as the super finished showing her mother how to ignite the pilot light under the stove. The gruffness he'd exhibited before seemed to be all gone now. He was friendly, almost bashful. Mrs. Madrid had this effect on people, Reina knew. "Everyone loves your mother," her father used to tell her.

"Yep, the pilot light is a tricky thing," the super said in a strong Queens accent, wiping his hands on his pants. It seemed like he was trying to prolong his visit. "Even for people who know stoves, pilot lights are tricky. But you're probably not that familiar with them, where you're from. Do they have stoves in your country?" It was asked innocently, without malice.

Mrs. Madrid smiled her charming smile. Reina could tell she thought the question was ridiculous.

"Yes" was all she answered.

"Of course they have stoves," Reina chimed in, annoyed that her mother didn't elaborate, didn't tell him that if she didn't know about "pilot lights," whatever those were, it wasn't because she'd never seen a stove before, but because she'd grown up with maids and cooks who did all the cooking in her house. "You should see the house she grew up in! It was big. It had marble floors."

"My husband is cook here" was all that Mrs. Madrid added.

"Huh, well, there you go," said the super, nodding awkwardly.

He finished, turned the knobs on all four burners to show them that the stove now worked, and accepted the glass of water Mrs. Madrid offered him. Then he left.

Reina did not ask her mother why she had made it seem like her father was still alive to the super. She knew. She had been in enough hospital rooms and lawyers' offices to understand the coded way adults talk, the way their mouths might say one thing but their eyes say another. She learned that a sentence like "I'm sure your dad will be fine" actually meant "Your dad is dying but you'll be fine." Or "Your mom's going to need you to be brave" meant "I don't want to deal with you crying right now, little girl." Reina had become very good at this language of Things Not Said. This was why she had become so indispensable to her mother in the months after her father's passing— she would translate not just the content but the intent of conversations that her mother couldn't follow. "No, *mami*, the lawyer didn't say *papi* didn't have any money, he said *papi* owed more money than he had, so that's why we're not getting anything."

In this way, Reina Madrid had become, very quickly, an equal partner in the new enterprise that was the Madrid family. Where before it had been her father and mother making all the big decisions together, now it was her and her mother. Where they should live. What they should do next. The two of them divided the work that had to be done, the things that Reina's father used to do for the family. Reina, for instance, was not only the translator now, but the map reader, the subway navigator, the appliance operator, the picture taker, and the game explainer. These were all things that her father used to do that Mrs. Madrid didn't do particularly well (in addition to cooking, baking, or sewing). The things Mrs. Madrid did do well were far less practical in nature. Storytelling. Dream deciphering. Mind reading. Added to these responsibilities were now sand-castle building, Easter egg painting, card playing, and driving (the latter only because Reina would not be able to do it for a good number of years). The thing Mrs. Madrid was best at, though—and this was something Reina would hear over and over again as she grew older—was her uncanny ability to make everyone she spoke to feel like there was nothing in the world they could not do. If you wanted to fly to the moon, Mrs. Madrid would help you build the spaceship. This was her greatest talent.

3.

Four years passed. In that time, Franny and Reina became true best friends. They knew each other's secrets, could make each other laugh with just a look. They negotiated well who would go first at this or that, and in all those years, they had never had a fight. Franny, who was a year older than Reina (which is why they never saw each other in school) went to Reina's house right after school every day. The two would sit side by side at the kitchen table and do their homework. Then, once they were both finished, they would go out and play until it was time for dinner. Most nights, Franny ate at Reina's house. On Friday nights, she almost always slept over on the little cot Mrs. Madrid would pull out from under Reina's bed. Saturday mornings they would watch cartoons until noon, eating breakfast brought to them in bed by Mrs. Madrid, whose one true cuisine was Aunt Jemima pancakes.

Later, Mrs. Madrid would take them to the movies or bowling. Sometimes, in the winter, they would go ice-skating. In the summer, Mrs. Madrid usually took them to the beach, or Adventurers Inn. Anyone who didn't know better would have thought they were sisters, the way Mrs. Madrid treated the two girls. Whatever she bought for Reina, she bought for Franny: stuffed animals at the carnival; ice skate pom-poms at the rink. Mrs. Madrid had gotten a job as a receptionist in the Spanish-language department of a nearby college. She earned enough money now that she could afford to spoil Reina the way she wanted to. This was why Reina had been the first in her neighborhood to get a five-speed Stingray, and the only one to go to Disney World. Mrs. Madrid was unapologetic about indulging her only daughter's wants and wishes, and if that meant paying for her daughter's best friend on all these adventures, she didn't mind. Reina didn't mind. And certainly Franny didn't seem to mind, either.

For a little while early in their best-friendship, Reina did wonder why she had never been invited for a sleepover at Franny's house, despite all the times Franny had slept over at her house. It didn't bother her, exactly, but it made her wonder. Then, one day when Franny was sick with the flu and had missed a couple of days of school, Reina brought her a jar of soup after school. She rang Franny's bell, expecting Franny's mom to come downstairs. But she was buzzed in, and walked upstairs and knocked on Franny's door. Franny opened the door, looking terrible, said her mother was at the drugstore, took the soup, coughed, thanked her, and then closed the door.

In that brief time, Reina glimpsed inside Franny's home and understood instantly why her best friend had never invited her over. Piles of clothes everywhere. Boxes and crates strewn all over the floor. It looked like a tornado had hit the apartment. It was the same size as the one-bedroom she and her mother shared, but it looked so different! How did five people live there? Franny, her sister and brother, their two parents? No wonder Franny didn't have friends over—there was no room!

Seeing Franny's apartment also helped explain a story Franny had once told her, which she had really never believed because it seemed so outrageous, but now made sense. Franny told her that she had once gotten locked inside her coat closet for twelve hours, and no one had even realized she was missing until her dad needed his jacket the next morning! She had pounded and pounded on the door, but between the TV blaring in the living room and her older brother blasting his music in the other room, no one heard her. Franny had told the story in such a funny way that Reina had laughed. They had both giggled when Franny imitated her dad's expression on finding her in the closet. But afterward, Reina could not stop thinking about how horrible it must have been to have gotten locked inside a closet and not have anyone know you were missing. She felt bad for Franny, though she never said anything. She liked that her own mother always kept close tabs on her, annoying as that could be sometimes. Even when her mother was at work, Reina had to check in with her.

Reina liked that her mother worked in an office and

had the kind of job where she had to wear nice clothes every day. None of the other moms in the neighborhood had jobs like that. Not Karen and Tommy's mom, who was kind of the Band-Aid mom in the neighborhood, the one whose apartment you went to if you scraped a knee and your own mom wasn't home. Not Debbie's mom, who was the wounded-creature mom. If you found a baby bird that had fallen out of its nest, you would take it to Debbie's mom, who was said to have once nursed an electrocuted squirrel back to health. Neither Josephine's mom, David's mom, nor Georgie's mom worked outside their homes, either. Roy Ponte's mom sold Tupperware, but worked from her home.

The only other mom who had an office job, besides Reina's mom, was Patty Perry's mom in building 3. Mrs. Perry worked in the city as a secretary at a big ad agency. She wore very fashionable clothes and had the brightest, yellowest hair Reina had ever seen. Perhaps because they were the only two single working moms in the neighborhood, or because they both had a certain glamour to them, Mrs. Perry and Mrs. Madrid had become close friends. By then, Mrs. Madrid was fluent enough in English that her sly humor could poke through (although her Spanish accent now had a distinctly Queens flavor to it). Despite her accent, or perhaps because it made her seem worldly and intriguing to the other moms on the block, Reina's mother was a greatly sought-after friend in the neighborhood.

The only mother Mrs. Madrid didn't become friends with, strangely enough, was Franny's mother, Mrs. Jones. The truth was, Franny's mom wasn't really friends with any of the other mothers in the neighborhood. On summer nights, when all of them brought out their lawn chairs to sit and chat in the courtyard while the kids caught fireflies, Mrs. Jones would say hello when she came to pick up her daughters, but she never joined them or lingered for longer conversations. Reina herself had only talked to Mrs. Jones a handful of times. As for Franny's dad, Mr. Jones, Reina had never—not even once—been introduced to him, or talked to him, or seen him up close. She'd spotted him from afar a few times, getting off the bus in his tweed cap, walking with his wife and children to church. But she'd never interacted with him. Not that she thought much of that. In those days, it was commonly accepted that most dads were only minimally involved in the day-to-day aspects of their kids' lives. Aside from an occasional football toss with the kids, or a swing of the stickball bat, dads were a distant and unapproachable phenomenon. To Reina, whose memories of her own dad were becoming a little fuzzy at the edges, there was no problem in accepting this blurry version of Franny's dad.

4.

The Fourth of July was everyone's favorite holiday, next to Christmas and Halloween. The big kids from a nearby neighborhood, led by the infamous Simone brothers, would put on a fireworks display from the roof of the tall building on 156th Street. Every year, rumors would circulate for days prior to the show about what kinds of fireworks would be displayed. There were rumors, too, that Eddie Simone had lost his right pinkie from a firecracker accident, which only added to the glamour of the spectacle.

No one went to sleepaway camp in Reina's neighborhood. Reina had heard about kids in school who went away for weeks on end, but it mystified her. Why would anyone choose to leave for the summer? Summer was a magical time. You got to go out all day long, play with your friends, stay out late as long as there was even a little bit of light in the sky. The days lasted forever. The kids cycled through new phases of things to do every week or so. One week they'd be setting up Evel Knievel stunt courses for their bikes in the courtyard. Another week they'd be making go-carts to push down the grassy slope in Kissena Park. Sometimes they played wild games like Ride the Pony, where somebody always got hurt. Sometimes they played Spud. Sometimes they'd put on shows for the moms, acting out Partridge Family songs in their bell-bottom pants.

For Reina, every day of summer started the same. A quick breakfast. Run down to Karen and Tommy's house on the first floor. Wait for them to get ready. Then the three of them would go "call for" the other kids in the neighborhood, one window at a time.

On July Fourth, Reina started early, tiny American flag in hand. After getting Tommy and Karen, who were also ready to go earlier than usual, the three trotted to Debbie's building first, since it was adjacent to theirs, rang the buzzer, and then waited below Debbie's third-floor kitchen window. All the windows on that side of the building were wide open, since most people, if they had an air conditioner, had it in their living room on the other side of the building. A few minutes later, Debbie's mom poked her head out the window. "She's brushing her teeth. She'll be down in a minute!" she called to the trio below.

"Happy Fourth of July!" Reina yelled, waving her tiny flag enthusiastically.

"You too, Reina!" Debbie's mom answered.

Two minutes later, Debbie came running outside, a smear of toothpaste on her cheek. The four then went to call for the next kid. It didn't take long for the group to grow to epic proportions, since everyone was ready to play as soon as they were called for. Josephine, David, Georgie, Kim, Marisa the new girl, Big Frank, Pete, Patty, Danny, and Roy Ponte, who alone among all of them lived in a house on 159th Street. It was a big crowd for so early in the morning. They were all giddy in anticipation of the day and, most especially, the night to come. They argued about what game to play on the way to call for Franny and Carol, the last stop before beginning their adventures. Somehow, punchball was settled on.

They rang the buzzer for 2D, and then waited outside the building entrance. Franny quickly came to the window.

"I'm almost finished with breakfast!" she called down, her mouth full.

"What about Carol?" Roy Ponte asked.

Franny's sister, Carol, was the prettiest girl on the block, and everyone knew she and Roy were starting to like each other.

"She can't come out till she does the dishes!" they heard Franny's mom yell from somewhere behind her. She sounded angry. They could hear a hint of turmoil coming from the house: voices yelling in another room.

"Hurry up, Franny!" someone called out, after they'd all been waiting a good five minutes.

No one liked to have to wait for too long. Waiting usually led to arguments in a crowd of kids this size. Someone in the group had already questioned whether punchball was the right game choice, and when Big Frank suggested ringalario, everyone razzed him mercilessly because it was common knowledge ringalario could only be played at dusk.

"Franny!" several other voices yelled up to Franny's empty kitchen window. "Hurry up!"

Reina was not one of these voices. She knew, or sensed, that Franny had other forces at work in her morning routine that had nothing to do with the kids below, and everything to do with the chaos inside her home. It wasn't uncommon for Franny to emerge from her building with mismatched sneakers, or a shirt worn inside out. There was always some waiting around for Franny. But today the crowd was ruthless.

"Come on, let's just go," said Kim, an older girl who didn't usually hang out with them.

"But she'll be down in a second," Reina said.

"We've been waiting forever," Kim said, clucking her tongue. "Let's just go, already!"

An argument was about to start, but luckily Franny came trotting out the front door of the building just in time. She seemed almost breathless.

"I'm ready!" she said, running past the group.

The crowd began to head toward the long courtyard, when a voice boomed from Franny's kitchen window. It was a man's voice, and it sounded like thunder.

"Franny, you get back here!" Franny's father yelled from the window.

The kids all stopped in their tracks and looked up. They could see Franny's dad, in his white undershirt, red-nosed, at the window looking down at them.

"I'm just playing for a little while!" Franny yelled back.

"I told you you're not going out and playing with that spic anymore!" he shouted.

There was silence. A silence like a cloud that consumed all the worldly sounds: no buses, no cars, no birds. Silence.

Reina was looking up like everyone else, not even realizing what he'd said at first. But then it hit her, quickly, with the strange clarity of a firework in the night, a Roman candle explosion in still black air: he was talking about her. None of these other kids spoke Spanish. She was the only one with the long black ponytail and the warm brown eyes. Her skin was the color of *canela,* as her mother used to say. Cinnamon. Later when she went to art school, she would learn the word *sepia* was the best color word to describe her. But for now, *canela.* Franny's father had just called her spic in front of all her neighborhood friends. It was an incandescent moment. It was a flash going off, obscuring vision.

No one looked at Franny, or Reina. The kids looked down at the sidewalk, or at each other. Reina didn't see Franny's expression as she ran back inside the building. She herself swallowed hard. It didn't occur to her to cry. She wasn't angry. She was embarrassed, though. She was still, like she was at the age of six, a very shy girl. She didn't like to be the center of attention.

Reina turned to Karen and Tommy, the kids she felt closest to, who knew her the best. Their eyes were wide, trying to gauge her expression to see how they should react. Reina thought they looked like they were waiting for her to speak, to say something, but she didn't want to. She found no words. She wanted the moment to be over, forgotten.

"Let's just play, already," said Roy Ponte, punching the Spalding ball into the courtyard.

The kids, as if released from a game of freeze tag, followed the ball into the courtyard. It bounced off the walls, and Roy caught it and called, "Captain." Big Frank called, "Captain!" They picked sides. Reina always got picked second or third. She was good at punchball.

Nothing was said about what had just happened. Reina, focused on the game, blew all thoughts of it away. She punched them away every time it was her turn at bat.

Franny didn't come back out to play that day. She didn't watch the fireworks that night. But she showed up the next day. No one called for her, but she came out and joined the group in the middle of a game of tag. She said hello to Reina as if nothing had happened, and Reina said hello to her. Neither one of them ever acknowledged what had happened. They were best friends, but they were strangers, too. There were boundaries, like in foreign countries, that were never crossed.

5.

Reina didn't tell her mother about the incident until the end of summer. Maybe she was afraid her mother wouldn't let her play with Franny anymore. Maybe she was afraid her mother's feelings would get hurt. But finally she told her mother one night as she was going to bed, as her mother sat on the side of the bed stroking her hair. Her mother didn't react the way she'd thought she would.

"Poor Franny," her mother said after a moment. "Imagine, growing up with such an ignorant father. He doesn't know you. He doesn't know me. Such an ignorant man. Did Franny ever say anything to you afterward?"

"No."

"Not surprising. What could she say, after all?"

Reina looked at her mother in the darkness.

"Is that it?" she said, relieved. "I thought you were going to tell me I couldn't play with her anymore or something."

"Why would I punish Franny by depriving her of your friendship?" her mother answered. "She needs you, Reina. She needs you much more than you need her. Years from now, when she looks back, she'll see the happiest days of her childhood involved being with you, going ice-skating, going to the beach, the pancakes in bed on Saturday mornings. She'll remember all that."

"Will she remember her father calling me a spic?"

"She'll never forget that, I'm sure. And neither will you. It will be a little line in the story of your life. But you'll have much bigger stories to write someday." Mrs. Madrid bent over and kissed her daughter on the forehead. "Now go to sleep, *mi reina bella, mi reina adorada.*"

Reina closed her eyes and turned on her side. She did not want her mother to see that she was crying. Not because of the horrible word uttered by a red-nosed man she would never see again. But because she knew her best friend would never have a mother like hers, or know the tenderness of that one luminous word uttered in the darkness: *reina.*

Go Fish

William Alexander

Colt, Elora, and Avery had never spoken to each other before they found the catacombs. They were neighbors, but
they didn't know each other's names. Colt was seven years
old, Elora eleven, and Avery thirteen. Those ages were separate nations whose citizens didn't really speak the same
language. But the catacombs gave them common ground
and something to talk about.

Colt found the place first. It was bedtime on an early
summer night. He had already had a bath. He had needed
that bath. Colt liked dirt. He'd spent the afternoon helping
ghosts in his backyard sculpt new and muddy bodies for
themselves. But now Colt was clean. He had brushed his
teeth and put on pajamas with feet attached. He had done
all the things he was supposed to do at bedtime—except

stay in bed. He couldn't sleep. He wasn't tired. So he snuck down to the basement, which was his favorite place.

Colt was pale, the sort of pale that sunburned easily and made his skin look like it belonged to a cave creature shut away from sunlight for several hundred thousand generations. But that wasn't why he loved the basement. He wasn't really a cave creature. He just had Viking ancestors. Not the warrior kind—Colt's people had never been any good at fighting. They were good at singing and catching fish. He knew this because some of his Viking ancestors haunted the bathtub and they still sang songs about catching fish.

The basement was Colt's favorite place because sound behaved strangely there. He hummed the songs of his fisherfolk ancestors and tapped out a drumbeat on the basement wall.

One part of the wall made a different sound from the rest. Colt tapped it again. Then he pushed. Something spring-loaded clicked on the other side. The whole wooden wall panel opened.

Colt was surprised. But a part of him had always expected to find a secret passage in his own basement. He took a camping lantern and went down into the catacombs.

The ghosts of that place were immediately worried about Colt, a young kid exploring in the dark all by himself.

Some of those ghosts still remembered their voices, so they sent whispers through the second tunnel and into Elora's basement.

Ana Maria, Elora's older sister, had set up her bedroom in the basement. But now Ana Maria was away at film school—even in summertime, because she had an internship—so Elora had claimed the entire basement as her own. She was dancing when she heard the whispers. She was usually dancing. No single spot on the ground was ever interesting enough to hold the attention of her feet.

The whispers told her about the wall panel, the one Ana Maria had covered up with movie posters. Elora took down the posters, pushed against the panel, and then went into the catacombs by the shining light of her phone.

The tunnel floor was made out of bricks in a zigzagging pattern. More bricks had been stacked to make the walls. Dirt, wooden rafters, living tree roots, and haunting ghosts made up the ceiling.

Elora found a wide-open room at the end of the tunnel.

A ghost with a lantern stood in that room.

Elora peered at him. "Wait. You're not dead."

"Nope," said Colt.

"You're the kid from down the street."

"I'm Colt Harper," said the kid.

"Elora Giselle Dulce," said Elora.

Colt held up the camping lantern to see his neighbor

more clearly. Elora was dark. People whose ancestors lived close to the equator were usually dark, for obvious reasons. They didn't sunburn easily. Elora's own ancestors came from an island that had sunk beneath the sea. Their ghosts also sang songs about fishing, but none of them haunted her bathtub. Elora's great-great-grandparents preferred to rest inside ice cube trays. Their music escaped whenever their ice melted in lemonade.

"Where are we?" Colt asked. "Why is there a secret door and a secret tunnel in my basement?"

Elora looked around by phone light. "I don't know. But I can see *three* tunnels. Plus a door. I wonder where they go." She tried the door. It was stuck. "Okay. Forget the door. Should we see whose basement the third tunnel connects to?"

"Maybe we shouldn't find out." Colt felt nervous for the first time since he had come down into the catacombs. "Maybe one of the mean kids at school lives at the other end. Maybe it's somebody we don't want to share a secret tunnel with."

"Maybe," Elora said. "But I'd rather know than just wonder and worry. If that tunnel does lead to someone else's house, then that someone could use it to sneak right into *our* houses whenever they want. And if one of the mean kids can do *that,* then I'd really like to know about the possibility before it happens."

Colt slowly nodded. "I guess that makes sense."

The two of them went through the third tunnel together. They found another wooden panel at the very end.

Elora knocked.

Avery Nook sat on the couch in the finished half of their half-finished basement, hard at work on a graphic novel about ghosts who knitted new bodies for themselves out of branches and belly button lint. Avery liked to knit almost as much as they liked to draw. Avery liked to keep their hands busy by making things.

The linty ghosts of the comic had adventures inside walls and huge hollow trees, where they fought battles against villainous woodchucks.

A knock came through the basement wall.

Avery wondered if the comic that they'd made up might be coming true. Maybe small and linty warriors were sending a summons to adventure. Probably not. But Avery shifted a big pile of boxes out of the way and listened to the wall, just to be sure. Their family had just moved into this house a month ago, so dozens of unpacked boxes were still scattered all over the place.

Knock knock knock.

"Hello?" Avery whispered.

Click. The wall opened. Two younger kids from down the way stood inside.

Avery felt simultaneously delighted and disappointed

that their visitors were not, in fact, tiny warriors made out of knitted twigs and lint.

The three made introductions.

"Are you a boy or a girl?" Colt blurted out. "I can't tell by your name." He couldn't tell by looking, either. Avery wore neither girlish nor boyish things. They had darkish skin that wouldn't sunburn too easily, massive glasses to better magnify their most intimidating stare, and short black hair that stuck out in all directions as though pointing to every continent where Avery's family had ever lived. Their people moved around a lot, and always had. Avery's ancestors didn't haunt this new house yet, though. Sometimes ancestry takes a while to catch up.

Avery tried to smile. A new neighborhood meant new rounds of tiresome explanations. It was like wearing a cast and having to answer the question *How did you hurt your arm?* several times daily.

"Yes and no," they said. "Both and neither. Don't call me he or she."

"Okay," said Colt.

"Come check out the big secret room," Elora said. "It's haunted, obviously, but just in the usual sort of way. The ghosts in the ceiling don't seem to mind company."

Avery wrote a hasty note on a blank page of the sketch pad and left it for their parents: OFF EXPLORING! BACK SOON.

✦ ✦ ✦

Colt and Elora showed Avery the chamber in the center of the catacombs. Haunting ghosts watched them from the dirt and roots above.

"Where does that door go?" Avery asked.

"Not sure," said Elora. "It's stuck."

The three of them pulled together, hard. The door creaked and then banged open. They found a long staircase on the other side. Avery led the way up.

The room at the top had been built out of polished granite blocks. It had old leaded windows and a big metal door, which was locked up tight. Moonlight shone in through the windows. Elora peered outside.

"We're in the town cemetery," she said. "This room must be a crypt. But it doesn't have a body in it. Weird. It hides the stairs to our basements instead."

Avery realized what the catacombs had to be.

"Prohibition tunnels!" they said. "Specialists used them in the 1920s when it was really illegal to talk to ghosts."

"What?" Colt asked, horrified. "Why would that be illegal?"

Avery shrugged. "Some people freak out about hauntings."

"Hauntings just get worse if you ignore them," Elora pointed out.

"Obviously," Avery said. "So all the appeasement specialists kept working. They just went underground. Literally underground. They made secret tunnels to all the cemeteries. Then the law got changed, because that law was a terrible idea in the first place. Now we have proper specialists who don't need to sneak around through tunnels."

"Some places have proper specialists," Elora said. "Here we've got Mr. Armstrong."

"Is he any good?" Avery asked.

Elora hesitated. "He's very nice. . . . The ghosts seem to like him."

"My mom says 'Bless his heart' a lot," Colt added.

"Crap," said Avery, who knew what that meant even though they weren't from around here. "Well, at least Mr. Armstrong doesn't have to hide."

Avery and Colt both stood close to Elora to look through the window. The moon made pale granite gravestones seem to glow. Wisp lanterns flickered from the tree branches. A whole flock of sleeping pigeons huddled together on top of a tall statue. The statue held a cavalry sword high as though ordering a courageous charge against villainous enemies.

Avery wondered who that statue was, but didn't ask.

Every night, all through the summer, the three neighbors met in the catacombs beneath the cemetery to play card games.

Go Fish was Colt's favorite.

Avery liked Psychic Lemur, which involved slapping and stealing the discard pile every time someone correctly guessed what the next card was going to be. Avery was best at guessing, but Elora had the fastest slap.

Her favorite game was one that she had invented herself.

"This is called Sleepsuits," she said. "It's a sleepover game."

"Are we sleeping here tonight?" Colt asked, suddenly worried.

"No," Elora assured him. "We aren't sleeping here. This is just the sort of game that you might play at a sleepover. In whispers. While hiding in the camping tent that you set up on the floor of your bedroom."

"Does it rain in your room?" Colt asked.

"Not usually," Elora told him. "But it did once. I found a seashell at the beach and brought it home. The shell remembered tropical storms. It kept sharing that memory with me, which flooded the whole house, so we had to take it back to the beach. We couldn't just mail it to my cousins, because the post office won't let you mail tropical storms. Dad was annoyed. Mom liked the excuse for another weekend trip, though. She likes to drive. Even in the rain."

"Did it rain inside the car?" Colt asked.

"No. Just outside. We taped the shell to the roof of the car."

"So how do we play Sleepsuits?" Avery disliked the whole concept of sleepover games, but tried not to show it.

Elora skillfully shuffled the deck. "We take turns picking cards. Any card. Just one. If you pick a diamond, then you have to tell us something that you wish for—as many wishes as the number on the card. Pick the four of diamonds, tell us four wishes. They can be silly wishes. But if it's a heart, you have to tell us about something that you really need. A club is a weapon, so share something that you'll fight for—or tell us about somebody that you want to fight against. And spades mean secrets. We'll bury those between us and promise to never, ever tell anyone else."

"I don't get this game," Colt said slowly.

"I get it," Avery said, "but I don't think I like it. What do face cards do?"

"Queens and kings can command somebody else to answer," Elora explained. "If you draw a queen, then you get to skip your turn and pass to the left. If you draw a king, then you pass to the right. The next player has to answer for you. If Colt drew the king of diamonds, then I would have to share a wish."

"And jacks?" Avery asked.

"Jacks are tricky," Elora said. "If you draw a jack, then you get to give a hint instead of a straight answer."

"I still don't get this game," said Colt.

"I'll go first," Elora said in a reassuring sort of way.

"Avery next. You'll understand by the time it's your turn."
She flipped over the top card. "Ace of spades. I need to
share a secret."

"Just one," Avery said. "That's easy."

"Secrets are still the most difficult suit." Elora thought
for a moment. She looked up in the direction of the ceiling,
but she wasn't really looking at the ghosts, who looked back
down at her. "Okay. Here's one. I was mad at my older sister,
Ana Maria. I don't remember why I was mad at her, but I
do remember what I did about it: I switched the salt and the
sugar in the kitchen. She put salt in her coffee. It tasted terrible. The ghost who haunts the bottom of that mug liked the
taste, though, or else it just thought that my sister's spit-take
was hilarious. Now every single drink it holds tastes salty,
no matter what kind of drink it is. We only ever use that
mug to gargle salt water when we get sore throats. And I've
never, ever told Ana Maria that I was the one who switched
the salt. It was her favorite mug. And that's my secret." She
passed the deck to Avery. "Your turn."

Avery turned over the ten of clubs.

"You've got to be kidding," they said. "Ten?"

Elora smiled. "Ten. Tell us ten things you'll fight for.
Take your time. They can be big epic fights, or petty little
fights, or anything in between."

"I'd fight to never have to play this game again,"
they said.

"That's one! You'd lose, though. Sleepsuits is my favorite. Now tell us nine more."

Avery tried to think of nine more fights, but they didn't have to. Loud thumping noises interrupted the game. Ghosts scattered. Loose dirt rained down from the ceiling.

Colt jumped to his feet. "What is that?"

"It's coming from up above," Avery said. "Let's check it out."

"You're just trying to hide from the ten of clubs," Elora complained.

"I'm *also* trying to hide from the ten of clubs. Come on."

They all hurried upstairs and peeked through the wavy glass window.

The statue in the center of the cemetery had walked away from its pedestal. Now it stomped around in solid bronze boots and swung its cavalry sword at the pigeons. Poor Mr. Armstrong was trying to appease the haunted thing, but he couldn't even get its attention.

"Ouch," Colt whispered as the dull sword ended a pigeon.

The statue was still causing a disturbance when the three neighbors met on the following night.

Avery sat crisscrossed on the floor with a heavy book in their lap. "I went to the library today," they said. "The statue is of somebody named Beauregard Errington Grizzle.

His ghost is probably the one haunting it. I found his biography, and it turns out that he was a ridiculously bad person. Listen to this: *General Grizzle had the curious habit of dueling with swans and geese at dawn every morning. He would wade into the river shallows where a large flock of the birds were wont to sleep. Once startled, the pugnacious fowl would arch their necks and flap their wings in a fearfully intimidating manner, at which point the general would laugh with delight and then cut off as many heads as he could reach. 'The graceful shape of their necks is an invitation to a beheading, one that I am simply unable to refuse,' he once wrote in a letter to his mother."*

"Ew," Elora said. "And he's still at it. Still killing birds. He's also tearing up the cemetery, knocking over grave markers and chasing all the pigeons around, even though they don't have such long and beheadable necks." All this enraged her. She had two pet parakeets at home.

"Why did he get a statue?" Colt asked. "If he was so terrible, why did anybody want to build him one?"

Avery flipped through the pages. "Beats me. If General Grizzle ever did anything righteous or good, this book doesn't mention it."

Bronze boots stomped overhead. Agitated ghosts dropped from the ceiling and shifted their shapes all over the floor. Colt took up handfuls of the haunted dirt and tried to soothe them by singing quiet lullabies.

"Ignore that tantruming statue," Elora said. "We have a

game to play. Avery, it's still your turn. You can even draw a new card. Try not to get another ten."

Avery drew the queen of diamonds, which clearly delighted them. "I get to pass! Colt, tell us a wish. Just one."

Colt stopped singing. The ghost in his hand had settled into a single, lumpy shape.

"I wish I had new sneakers," he said. "Mine are too tight and my toes get scrunched up. It hurts."

"Have you told your parents?" Elora asked.

"No," Colt said. "I keep forgetting. So I also wish I had some string. I'd tie a piece around my toe to remind it that it doesn't like to get scrunched, and then maybe I'd remember to say that I need new shoes."

"I'll bring some string tomorrow," Elora told him. "My turn." She reached for the deck, but she paused when loud shouting noises came through the stairwell.

"Is that the statue?" Colt asked. "Doesn't sound like the statue. Sounds like a huge crowd of people."

It turned out to be two huge crowds of people.

Colt, Elora, and Avery crept up the stairs and peeked through the crypt window. They saw grown-ups gathered into two shouting groups. The noise disturbed dozens of cemetery ghosts, who swirled around in circles and threw pebbles at each other. Mr. Armstrong, the specialist, also ran in circles. He frantically pleaded with the ghosts. A pebble whacked his nose.

The haunted statue had returned to his pedestal, but didn't stand in his old heroic posture. Instead he sat with his back to the arguing crowds. A pigeon landed on top of his big bronze hat. The statue tried and failed to shoo it away.

"What are they arguing about?" Colt whispered.

The next day Elora grilled her parents about the cemetery protests, and that night she told the others what she had learned. She also remembered to bring some string and gave it to Colt. He tied it around his toe.

"Some people want to remove the statue," Elora said. "They say it never should have been built in the first place. But it's hard to remove a *haunted* statue. They would need to catch it first and coax the ghost somewhere else. That's some tricky appeasement. Mr. Armstrong probably can't manage it."

"What about the *other* group of marching, shouting people?" Avery wanted to know.

Elora's face took on a blank and neutral expression, which was odd. Her feelings were usually obvious. "The other group won't let Mr. Armstrong even try to bring the statue down. They say that we must continue to honor General Beauregard Errington Grizzle because he is a part of our history and heritage."

Her quiet tone of voice still made it absolutely clear what she thought of the second group.

"He's a pretty icky part of history," Avery said while furiously knitting a scarf.

"Do you have any sevens?" Colt asked. He didn't want to talk about this anymore. He just wanted to play cards.

Avery stopped knitting and handed over a seven.

"Do *you* have any sevens?" Colt asked Elora.

"No," said Elora. "Go fish."

They had already tried to play Psychic Lemur, but none of them could concentrate on complicated games with protests and counterprotests still shouting overhead. Sleepsuits was out of the question. Elora was still annoyed that they hadn't even finished a single round.

The ghosts of the catacombs began to panic. Those who had no voices made silent, wailing mouths, collapsed into mounds of loose dirt, and then remade themselves to wail silently again.

Elora stood.

"That's it," she said. "I've had enough. Colt, you've obviously got the most sensitive ears. Tell me where the statue is stomping right now."

Colt listened. He pointed. "There."

"Okay. Good." Elora shooed her two neighbors away from that spot. "The ghosts in the dirt listen to you. Especially when you sing lullabies. Sing them a song now.

Ask them to all move away from this place. Avery, you like trees. Talk to the roots. Try to get them to move, too."

"How do you know how much I like trees?" Avery asked. None of their Sleepsuits confessions had been about trees.

"Because you draw trees in your comic, and because you're knitting a tree pattern into your scarf right now. So talk to them."

Avery talked to the tree roots in a low whisper.

Colt sang to all the haunting ghosts who roiled through the cemetery dirt.

Root and soil moved aside. They shifted old coffins out of the way. A gaping hole opened in the ceiling of the catacombs, and the surprised statue of Beauregard Errington Grizzle came tumbling through it.

Soil and root knitted back together, closing up the hole.

The two shouting crowds didn't even notice when the subject of their disagreement suddenly disappeared. Mr. Armstrong, the bewildered specialist, saw it happen, but he never told anyone else what he had seen.

Avery, Colt, and Elora all felt very proud of what they had just accomplished. They also instantly regretted bringing an unstable and swan-slaughtering metal swordsman into their secret clubhouse.

Elora swallowed the taste of fear and bile before she stepped forward to address the statue.

"I wish that my hometown had known better than to ever build you in the first place," she said. "But we didn't know better. We built you anyway. Now we need you gone. Your fights are over. All of them. Including the one you keep picking with birds. Now, stay here. Stay secret. Stay buried for the next hundred years at least. Go stand in the corner and think hard about what you've done."

The statue lowered his sword.

"Thank you," said a booming bronze voice. "In life I thought everyone else was a ghost, and I myself the only truly living man in all the world. I was the only one capable of action, the only one deserving of worthy consideration. I exulted in that. In death I was rewarded with the same solitude, set high above all others and venerated for my own delusional cruelty. This town is proud of me, though I was the worst of its sons. I could not convince them that their pride had been misplaced. Thank you for delivering me from this high regard. And from the pigeons. Every day those birds left goopy waste all over my shoulders and hat."

Elora nodded as though she had never doubted that the statue would listen to her.

"Good," she said. "You'll be safe here from pigeon poop."

The statue lumbered into the farthest corner of the room and stood perfectly still.

Elora sat, collected all the scattered cards, and started to shuffle them.

"Do you think he'll really stay put?" Avery whispered.

"Yes," Elora said. "If he doesn't, we can just call down more dirt to bury him completely." She slapped the deck of cards on the ground between them and then drew the ace of spades again. "The statue is our secret. Your turn, Avery. We're going to finally finish this game."

About the Authors

William Alexander writes science fiction and fantasy for middle-grade audiences. His novels include *Goblin Secrets, Ghoulish Song, Ambassador, Nomad, A Properly Unhaunted Place,* and *A Festival of Ghosts.* Honors include the National Book Award, the Eleanor Cameron Award, two Junior Library Guild selections, an International Latino Book Award finalist, and the Earphones Award for audiobook narration. Will studied theater and folklore at Oberlin College, English at the University of Vermont, and creative writing at the Clarion Workshop. He teaches at the Vermont College of Fine Arts program in Writing for Children and Young Adults. Visit goblinsecrets.com for more.

Joseph Bruchac is a writer and traditional storyteller who lives in the Adirondack Mountains region of northern New York. Much of his work is inspired by his Native American (Abenaki) ancestry. He is the author of over 130 books for young readers and adults. His experiences include running a college program in a maximum security prison, teaching in West Africa, and doing wildlife rehabilitation with his wife, Nicola Marae Allain. His most recent novels are *Two Roads* and *Sasquatch and the Muckleshoot*. A former varsity wrestler at Cornell University, he received his black belt in Brazilian jiu-jitsu in 2018.

Anna Dobbin grew up reading stories written by her awesome mom (and now coauthor), Linda Sue Park. After college, Anna worked in the children's division of a major publishing company. Now she is a freelance copy editor and gets to work on all different types of projects, from young adult fiction to cookbooks to graphic novels. When she isn't writing or editing, Anna loves to travel, make (and eat) baked goods, and Instagram photos of her dog. She lives in Connecticut.

Lamar Giles writes novels and short stories for teens and adults. He is the author of the Edgar Award nominees *Fake ID* and *Endangered, Overturned,* and *Spin,* as well as the middle-grade fantasy *The Last, Last Day of Summer.* He is a founding member of We Need Diverse Books and a faculty member in the Spalding University MFA program. He resides in Virginia with his wife, Adrienne. Check him out online at lamargiles.com, or follow @LRGiles on Twitter.

Mike Jung is the author of *Geeks, Girls, and Secret Identities; Unidentified Suburban Object;* and *The Boys in the Back Row.* He's also contributed essays to the anthologies

Dear Teen Me, Break These Rules, 59 Reasons to Write, and *(Don't) Call Me Crazy.* His books have been honored by the Bank Street College of Education, the Children's Book Council Reading Beyond List, the Cooperative Children's Book Center, the Georgia Children's Book Awards, the Iowa Children's Choice Awards, the Kansas State Reading Circle, the National Parenting Product Awards, the Parents' Choice Foundation, and the Texas Bluebonnet Awards. Mike is a founding member of We Need Diverse Books and lives in the San Francisco Bay Area with his family.

Hena Khan grew up with her nose in a book. The stories she connected with as a child left a huge impression on her, and she still thinks of the characters, feelings, and random tidbits that she absorbed years ago. That's why she loves writing for kids—in the hopes that they'll read something she wrote more than once, and let it become part of who they are. Hena enjoys writing for all ages and exploring her Pakistani American culture, along with space, spies, and other topics. *Amina's Voice,* her recent middle-grade novel, was named a Best Book of the Year by the *Washington Post,* NPR, *Kirkus Reviews,* and others. She also wrote the Zayd Saleem: Chasing the Dream series: *Power Forward, On Point,* and *Bounce Back,* and several picture books, including *Golden Domes and Silver Lanterns, Night of the Moon, It's Ramadan, Curious George, Crescent Moons and Pointed Minarets,* and *Under My Hijab.*

Juana Medina was born and raised in Bogotá, Colombia. She is the author and illustrator of the Pura Belpré Award–winning chapter book *Juana & Lucas.* Juana is also the author and illustrator of *Juana & Lucas: Big Problemas, 1 Big Salad, ABC Pasta,* and *Sweet Shapes.* She illustrated *Smick!* by Doreen Cronin, *Lena's Shoes Are Nervous* by Keith Calabrese, and *I'm a Baked Potato!* by Elise Primavera. Juana has been lucky to earn recognitions from the Colombian Presidency, the National Cartoonists Society, the National Headliner Awards, the International Latino Book Awards, and even the Ridgway Award—which is quite impressive for someone who was a less-than-stellar student and who often got in trouble for drawing cartoons of her teachers. Despite all the trouble caused, Juana studied and taught at the Rhode Island School of Design (RISD) and the Corcoran School of the Arts and Design (where students had plenty of chances to draw cartoons of her). She lives with her wife, their twin sons, and their dog, Rosita. Visit her at juanamedina.com.

Ellen Oh is CEO of We Need Diverse Books (WNDB), a nonprofit organization dedicated to increasing diversity in children's literature. A former adjunct college instructor and corporate attorney, she is the author of the middle-grade novels *Spirit Hunters* and *Spirit Hunters: The Island of Monsters,* and the Prophecy young adult (YA) fantasy trilogy. She is the editor of WNDB's middle-grade anthology *Flying Lessons and Other Stories* and the YA anthology *A Thousand Beginnings and Endings*. Ellen lives with her husband and three children. You can visit her online at ellenoh.com.

R. J. Palacio is the daughter of Colombian immigrants and is a first-generation American. She is also the author of the #1 *New York Times* bestselling middle-grade novel *Wonder,* as well as the other titles in the Wonder universe, including *365 Days of Wonder: Mr. Browne's Book of Precepts, Auggie & Me,* and *We're All Wonders.* Her first graphic novel, *White Bird, A Wonder Story,* which she both wrote and illustrated, will be published in 2019. She lives in Brooklyn, New York, with her husband, two sons, and their two dogs. You can find her online at wonderthebook.com.

Linda Sue Park is the author of the Newbery Medal winner *A Single Shard* and the *New York Times* bestseller *A Long Walk to Water,* as well as many other books for young readers. Her most recent titles are the Wing & Claw fantasy trilogy; *Fatal Throne,* a YA collaborative novel; and *Gondra's Treasure,* a picture book about a mixed-race dragon. She loves to read, travel, cook, eat, knit, watch baseball and movies, and play games on her phone. Linda Sue feels very fortunate that her family of heroes includes her daughter,

Anna Dobbin, with whom she sometimes collaborates on writing projects.

Olugbemisola Rhuday-Perkovich is the author of *8th Grade Superzero,* which was named a Notable Book for a Global Society and a Notable Social Studies Trade Book for Young People. She also writes nonfiction, including *Above and Beyond: NASA's Journey to Tomorrow* and *Someday Is Now: Clara Luper and the 1958 Oklahoma City Sit-Ins*, a Notable Social Studies Trade Book for Young People. She is the coauthor of the middle-grade novel *Two Naomis,* which was nominated for an NAACP Image Award and is a Junior Library Guild selection, and its sequel, *Naomis Too,* a Nerdy Book Club winner. She is a member of the Brown Bookshelf and a former We Need Diverse Books board member. She has contributed to numerous anthologies for children, teens, and educators, holds an MA in education, and writes frequently on literacy-related topics for Brightly. Visit her online at olugbemisolabooks.com.

Cynthia Leitich Smith is the *New York Times* and *Publishers Weekly* bestselling, award-winning author of *Jingle Dancer, Indian Shoes, Rain Is Not My Indian Name,* and other critically acclaimed books, poems, and short stories for kids and teens.

She is a citizen of the Muscogee (Creek) Nation and

teaches on the faculty of the MFA in Writing for Children & Young Adults program at Vermont College of Fine Arts. Cynthia also is on the Honorary Advisory Board of We Need Diverse Books. She makes her home in Austin, Texas, and the Austin chapter of the Society of Children's Book Writers and Illustrators has instituted the Cynthia Leitich Smith Mentor Award in her honor. Her upcoming books are prose and graphic-format novels for middle-grade readers.

Ronald L. Smith is the Coretta Scott King/John Steptoe Award–winning author of *Hoodoo,* which also received the 2016 ILA Award for Intermediate Fiction.

His other books include *Black Panther: The Young Prince* and *The Mesmerist,* a supernatural Victorian fantasy. His latest middle-grade novel is *The Owls Have Come to Take Us Away.*

Suma Subramaniam is a writer by night, and hires skilled technical professionals for a leading software company during the day. She's also an editor at Angelella Editorial and contributes to fromthemixedupfiles.com. Suma is a member of the Internship Grants team at We Need Diverse Books. She is also mentorship coordinator for the Society of Children's Book Writers and Illustrators (SCBWI–Western Washington Chapter). She holds an MFA in Writing from

Vermont College of Fine Arts, a certificate in popular fiction from the University of Washington, and advanced degrees in computer science and management.

Rita Williams-Garcia is the celebrated author of ten novels for young adults and middle-grade readers. Her most recent novel, *Clayton Byrd Goes Underground,* won an NAACP Image Award for Outstanding Literary Work—Youth/Teens and was a National Book Award finalist. She is best known for her Coretta Scott King Author Award–winning Gaither Sisters trilogy, which begins with *One Crazy Summer.*

About We Need Diverse Books

In the spring of 2014, We Need Diverse Books (WNDB) began as a simple hashtag on Twitter. Five years later, WNDB has grown from a grassroots movement into a non-profit organization, with a team that spans the globe. We are writers and illustrators, editors and agents, book bloggers and book lovers, all united under the same goal—to create a world in which every child can see themselves in the pages of a book. As we make our way in this often-troubled world, WNDB clings passionately to the active hope of award-winning author and advocate Walter Dean Myers, who wrote to make sure that we see each other, that we "explore our common humanity" and create new stories, together.

WNDB runs ten groundbreaking initiatives, including the annual Walter Dean Myers Award for Outstanding Children's Literature, which honors the legacy of Myers. In a 2014 *New York Times* essay, Myers wrote that he "found who I was in the books that I read." Myers understood that "books transmit values. They explore our common humanity. What is the message when some children are not represented in those books?" WNDB understands that "there is work to be done," and through programs and projects like the Walter Grants, which offer financial support to emerging children's writers and illustrators; WNDB in the Classroom, which sends thousands of books to schools in need; and the Internship Grant Award program, which offers support to a diverse cadre of interns working at publishing houses and literary agencies, we continue to build upon that work.

WNDB believes that all our voices matter, that each of our stories is a treasure. We know that reading promotes empathy and builds understanding across boundaries and borders. This is our third anthology, and it is a testament and tribute to that real power you have, each and every one of you who picks up this book. When Walter Dean Myers wrote, he wrote to gift readers with "the recognition of themselves in the story, a validation of their existence as human beings, an acknowledgment of their value by someone who understands who they are." Just by reading and sharing this book, you become a part of this important work. WNDB sees you, we believe in you, in the small, good things you do every day. We celebrate the ways you allow your unique story to become your superpower. We are listening to you. We write for you. And we want you to write back, in the way that's most truly *you*.

Myers wrote to make all children "feel as if they are part of America's dream, that all the rhetoric is meant for them, and that they are wanted in this country." All of us can work to fulfill the promise of "liberty and justice for all." How can we move ourselves, and each other, forward? How can you take the hand of that person right beside you, that person with their own story that maybe you don't recognize at first, that story that feels unfamiliar and a little itchy until you remember that everyone brings something special and necessary to this universe?

Who are your heroes next door? What can you do to bring out the hero inside of you? Together, we can transform the world of children's literature, and beyond.

Visit diversebooks.org to start now.